PUFFIN BOOKS

'How do I tell you this story?
Do I tell you the truth, the whole truth
and nothing but the truth?
Do I tell you my side or his?
What if I had been born on his side and
he on mine?
We were both only children . . .'

Beverley Naidoo grew up in South Africa under apartheid. She says: 'As a white child I didn't question the terrible injustices until I was a student. I decided then that unless I joined the resistance, I was part of the problem.' Beverley Naidoo was detained without trial when she was twenty-one and, in the following year, came into exile in England where she has since lived. Her first children's book, *Journey to Jo'burg*, was banned in South Africa until 1991, but it was an eye-opener for hundreds of thousands of readers elsewhere. In *Chain of Fire*, *No Turning Back* and *Out of Bounds* (short stories with a Foreword by Archbishop Tutu) there are extraordinary challenges for young people, black and white, caught in an oppressive society that she describes as 'more dangerous than any fantasy'. She has won many awards for her writing, including the prestigious Carnegie Medal and the Nestlé Smarties Silver Award for *The Other Side of Truth* about two refugee children smuggled to London who also feature in *Web of Lies*. She has written picture books and plays, and has two honorary doctorates as well a doctorate in education.

beverleynaidoo.com

Books by Beverley Naidoo

Burn My Heart
Chain of Fire
Journey to Jo'Burg
No Turning Back
Out of Bounds
The Other Side of Truth
The Great Tug of War
Web of Lies

To the Wefings

BEVERLEY NAIDOO

Let's cross
boundaries
of heart
and mind—

Burn *my* **heart**

Beverley Naidoo

PUFFIN

To the wefings.
Thanks for visiting us
in London. It meant the
world to us! ♡ Lucy

PUFFIN BOOKS

Published by the Penguin Group
Penguin Books Ltd, 80 Strand, London WC2R ORL, England
Penguin Group (USA) Inc., 375 Hudson Street, New York, New York 10014, USA
Penguin Group (Canada), 90 Eglinton Avenue East, Suite 700, Toronto, Ontario, Canada M4P 2Y3
(a division of Pearson Penguin Canada Inc.)
Penguin Ireland, 25 St Stephen's Green, Dublin 2, Ireland (a division of Penguin Books Ltd)
Penguin Group (Australia), 250 Camberwell Road, Camberwell, Victoria 3124, Australia
(a division of Pearson Australia Group Pty Ltd)
Penguin Books India Pvt Ltd, 11 Community Centre, Panchsheel Park,
New Delhi – 110 017, India
Penguin Group (NZ), 67 Apollo Drive, Rosedale, North Shore 0632, New Zealand
(a division of Pearson New Zealand Ltd)
Penguin Books (South Africa) (Pty) Ltd, 24 Sturdee Avenue, Rosebank,
Johannesburg 2196, South Africa

Penguin Books Ltd, Registered Offices: 80 Strand, London WC2R ORL, England

penguin.com

First published 2007
4

Set in Baskerville MT
Typeset by Palimpsest Book Production Limited, Grangemouth, Stirlingshire
Made and printed in England by Clays Ltd, St Ives plc

British Library Cataloguing in Publication Data
A CIP catalogue record for this book is available from the British Library

ISBN: 978-0-141-32124-0

For Muiruri and Gabriel
and a new generation who may want to know

Gũtirĩ ũkinyaga mũkinyĩre wa ũngĩ . . .
Nobody walks with another person's gait.

Contents

'If you don't stop that, the Mau Mau will come to get you!'

Anyone who was a child in Britain in the 1950s will probably remember hearing about the Mau Mau. The stories were frightening and, yes, some parents used the name as a threat . . . even though the Mau Mau were 4,000 miles away in Kenya.

These two words that alarmed many people in Britain, for at least ten years, then seem to have disappeared. They no longer made news. They hardly appeared even in history books. So what was this all about? Why the silence? With the scent of something secret, the detective in me became curious. I grew up in South Africa, 2,000 miles further south of Kenya, and there too we had many secrets.

So just a few words of history before the story begins . . .

Many Africans fought alongside British soldiers during the Second World War. Many of them died in the name of freedom. After the war, Africans declared that it was about time that they had their own freedom in their own countries. But the white settlers in Kenya refused even to share power. These wazungu, as they were called by Africans (mzungu for one white person), demanded that the country stay in

British hands. They insisted that Africans were like children, not ready for independence. When the African leader Jomo Kenyatta called for land, education, freedom, decent wages and equality, they called him a dangerous agitator. To most settlers, 'good' Africans were those who were loyal to them and the colony.

Kikuyus led the fiercest resistance. It was their fertile land in the highlands that the wazungu had taken for their farms. Many younger Kikuyus became impatient with older leaders like Kenyatta. They wanted action. A movement grew that became known as the Mau Mau. It was a secret society whose members took oaths and swore to fight unto death to get back their land. Any Kikuyu who was seen to help the white settlers was hated as much as the 'uninvited guests'. This story begins in the year before the State of Emergency. While the setting is real, my characters are all imagined.

I

'It's our secret, hey?'

'The fence is broken! Over here, Mugo!'

Mathew lifted the straggling barbed wire with the barrel of his gun. The other end remained attached to one of Father's new wooden posts. It was the bottom strand nearest the ground. Above it, row upon row of barbed wire stretched taut and intact, almost twice his height, between him and the bush. The new fence felt like a cage. The old fence had only reached his chest and its sagging wires had been easy for him and Mugo to push apart. Weak like old skin, Mugo had once said.

Careful not to touch the barbs, Mathew pinched the wire between his finger and thumb. He studied it. It hadn't come loose by itself. The other half hung from the adjoining post. It had been split in the middle. Sensing an adventure, Duma barked. Before he thought to stop her, Duma had stretched herself out and snuffled her way through the gap.

From the other side, she wagged her long copper tail at Mathew like a crazy feather duster. It would be difficult for a grown person to slip underneath. If the wire had been deliberately cut, why only the bottom wire?

Mathew squatted, his new Red Ryder rifle tucked under his arm. The blue-steel barrel of the gun pointed down. The hard tawny earth gave nothing away, or had Duma already swept away the evidence? Mathew frowned up towards Mugo, his speckled green eyes squinting against the sun.

'See any tracks?'

Mugo's jet-black eyes scoured the clumps of rough grey grass either side of the fence before he shook his head.

'Hapana . . . nothing.'

Mathew trusted Mugo's eyes to pick out the tiniest detail. Mugo was already thirteen, two years older than Mathew. His name even meant 'seer'. Before coming to work in the kitchen, he had been a herd boy. He knew all about the surrounding bush beneath their mountain.

'What did it, Mugo? An animal?'

'Hapana.' No. Not animal. Mugo shook his head again.

'People?'

Mugo said nothing. In the sun his cheeks glistened like the smooth polished walnut stock of Mathew's gun. But his forehead creased with worry lines.

Mathew followed the direction of Mugo's gaze to a whistling thorn tree on the other side of the fence. Had something snagged there on one of its long jagged spikes?

'I'm going to see,' Mathew announced.

Mugo sprang to life. 'Hapana, young bwana! Your father will be angry!'

'I'm only going to those trees.'

'Hapana! We must tell the bwana about the fence!' Mugo urged.

'He's gone out, Mugo,' Mathew retorted impatiently.

'Then we must tell –'

'Juma? His mother is sick and he's gone to see her. Father said he could.' Juma was Father's new foreman. Mathew grinned rather smugly. 'Don't worry, Mugo! We'll sort it out.'

'We can tell my father!' Mugo argued earnestly. He pointed to the blue gum trees in the direction of the stables, his fingers jabbing the air as if shocked by a bolt of electricity. Mugo's father, Kamau, was in charge of the stables.

'We'll do that but we've plenty of time to get someone to mend it before tonight. I just want to check if something's there.'

Before Mugo could reply, Mathew pushed his gun through the gap in the fence, flattened himself and began crawling. As long as he didn't go far and stay too long, why should Father ever know? He felt a little surge of pleasure at his defiance.

The bush on the other side was part of their land, all the way to the river. It extended far downstream into the plains and upstream through the thickly wooded lower slopes of Mount Kenya. 'Grayson country', as Mathew's grandfather used to call it. According to his mother, even as a toddler, Mathew used to beg the ayah who looked after him to let him go into the bush. However, her instructions were to keep him inside the fence. But by the time he was four, Mathew had latched on to Kamau who was responsible for Father's white stallion and who had worked on the Grayson farm since he was a boy himself.

With young Mathew's nagging and begging, Kamau was given permission to lead the child on a pony to the nearest stretch of river when he wasn't too busy. When Mathew could manage the pony himself, Kamau would ride beside him. One of his best feelings in the world was being perched at the top of the ridge early in the morning from where the two of them would watch wildlife come to drink in the water below. Kamau knew every animal and Mathew had never tired of listening to his stories.

Kamau's younger son, Mugo, had been one of the Grayson's herd boys until the day he had saved

Mathew from a deadly snake. Mathew, then six, had been with Father on his rounds to check that all the cattle were fenced inside the bomas before sundown. They had to be kept safe at night from lions and hyenas, even the occasional leopard from the mountain. Mathew had found an anthill near the entrance to a boma and begun poking it with a stick. Suddenly a black mamba had slithered out, rearing its head. If sharp-eyed Mugo hadn't yanked him away, its poison could have killed him within minutes. Father had praised Mugo for reacting so smartly and, soon afterwards, he was brought to work in the Grayson's kitchen.

In time, Mathew persuaded his parents to let him go into the nearby bush just with Mugo. That is whenever Josiah the cook would release him. Josiah used to grumble but usually gave in, especially after Mathew was sent to boarding school and only came home for holidays. At school, he would often lie awake in his narrow dormitory bed, planning expeditions with Mugo. Those plans helped him get through the long weeks away from home.

But recently things had begun to change. His father had said that Mathew wasn't to go out into the bush without him. It was a 'precaution'. Like his father always being armed these days . . . and now there was this new fence. Mother had only informed him about it in the car yesterday, on the way home from school for the weekend. There was nothing special to worry about, she had reassured. Their area was still quite peaceful. '*We're just being careful,*' Father had added. '*Those agitators won't get far here! I've always looked after my labour well so they're loyal. They won't want to upset the apple cart for themselves!*'

Mathew pulled himself up to his feet on the other side of the fence. Duma shook herself with delight as Mathew raised his Red Ryder like a commando.

'Come on!' he called to Mugo. 'I need you over here.'

Mugo continued to look unhappy and sighed loudly enough for Mathew to hear. However, he removed the red fez from his head and pulled off his white tunic. He folded the tunic with care before placing it on a tree stump with the fez on top. Sensible Mugo! Mathew knew how Josiah would berate the boy if there were just a spot on his uniform. He glanced down at his own dust-smeared shirt and trousers. Josiah's wife, Mercy, would grumble and tut-tut at him, but that would be all. She took such pride in returning his clothes freshly washed and pressed that he was sure her gripes were only show.

Mathew watched Mugo's muscles flex as he edged his body under the barbed wire. Duma was ecstatic at the adventure, sniffing at Mugo, glancing up at Mathew, and barking.

'Shh, Duma! Quiet, girl!'

It was broad daylight so it couldn't be that dangerous in the bush near to the fence. All the same, when Duma quietened down and Mugo was at his side, Mathew felt safer. He ignored the concern written across Mugo's face.

'I'll look for tracks this way. You go that!' Mathew pointed his two index fingers at right angles. 'We'll just go as far as those thorns over there so I still see you. Then we walk towards each other, swap over and come back, OK?'

Mugo frowned and remained silent.

'Oh, buck up, Mugo! Don't be such a wet blanket! I'm going anyway.'

As Mathew set off, Duma's lean copper face swung from one boy to the other. Her dark, elegant eyes looked worried.

'Here, Duma, here!' Mathew patted his thigh. But as Mugo started to walk, she padded after him.

Mathew let her go. He needed to concentrate if he was going to find any evidence of whoever might have cut their fence. If his detective work paid off and he had to admit breaking the new rule, surely Father wouldn't be too upset? He was actually pretty fed up with Father. For weeks he had been looking forward to going out hunting with him today. Whenever he had felt miserable at school, he had cheered himself up thinking about it. Father had promised that he could try out his new Red

Ryder properly. He had already spent hours assembling it, cleaning it, and learning to align the sights. He had practised its lightning loader and repeater action on targets far away from the house. He had also brought down a couple of chirpy bulbuls that had been eating fruit in Mother's orchard. But today was meant to be the first time he could try out the gun on something bigger. That was until Father had been called away to fix a neighbour's generator. *'Sorry, son, it has to take priority!'* It seemed to Mathew that other things always took priority.

He set off now, using the Red Ryder barrel to probe clumps of grass as he studied the earth for any tracks. His eyes also veered over nearby bushes and thorn trees for any giveaway signs. Every now and again, he looked across to check how Mugo and Duma were doing. Boy and dog were working as a team. Mathew felt a pang of jealousy. Duma was *his* dog. She had come to him as a longhaired red setter puppy. He had named her. It wasn't that she looked much like a cheetah – 'duma' in Swahili – but because he wanted her to be the fastest dog in the world! He was older now and knew she would never qualify for that title, but he loved her dearly. When he first had to leave her to spend weeks away at school, he had cried bitterly and, to his shame, had wet his dormitory bed. Matron hadn't been pleased, especially when under interrogation, and in tears, he had revealed that he was missing his dog. '*If you'd been weeping for your mother, I might understand!*' she had scolded in her Scottish 'no-nonsense' accent.

Mathew had almost reached the cluster of thorn trees, when a flicking caught his eye between the sprawl of branches ahead. He stopped dead still. The flicking had stopped. He held his breath, then released it gently when he saw that it was only an impala. However, when the buck lifted its head and turned to look at him, he was spellbound. It was a grown male with a magnificent set of curving, curling horns! Perhaps longer than his arms! The buck remained perfectly still, the black tips on its white ears primed liked antennae.

Trying not to tremble, Mathew slowly raised his rifle. This was his chance! What a trophy, if only . . .! He pressed the stock under his armpit, brought his left eye in line with the barrel while crooking his left forefinger round the trigger. But before he could squeeze the trigger, the buck swung its head and fled. At the same moment, Duma barked, rushing across the long grass ready to chase. Mathew called her to heel.

'Silly girl!' he said crossly. 'I almost got him!' He wasn't sure who had broken the spell, Duma or the impala. Either way he had lost his moment. But, maybe all wasn't lost. Mathew turned to Mugo, who had followed Duma.

'Let's go to the ridge! We'll see everything from there.'

'Hapana, young bwana! It's not safe! We must go back.' Mugo's pitch rose.

But Mathew's nerves were tingling. How could he give up the prize when it was so close? The impala could be drinking at the river. To go to the ridge wouldn't be that much further. He and Mugo had been there countless times. He ejected the straggling barbed wire from his mind.

'You're over-reacting because of the new fence, Mugo. Even Mother says it is only a precaution. Follow me!' Mathew ordered.

It was roughly the same distance as they had already covered from the fence. Mathew was tempted to run, but Father's voice in his head restrained him. '*Don't run with a gun.*' It was also stupid to think he could ever keep up with the impala. As long as the impala didn't feel it was being chased, it might stay near the river.

Mathew kept to the open grass with the thicket of thorns on their right. Despite shaking his head, Mugo had followed. This time, Duma obstinately pushed to the front.

'Don't you dare bark this time!' Mathew whispered. Duma cocked her head with an offended 'Do you think I'm that stupid?'.

Mathew strained to keep inspecting the ground ahead as well as constantly skimming his eyes in a hundred-and-eighty-degrees arc. When the undergrowth thickened beneath the thorn trees on their right, he was aware of a little nagging voice inside him: '*Give up! Anything – or anyone – could be in there!*' But Mugo was right behind him, wasn't he? Mugo knew the bush like the back of his hand. Mugo was surely only worried because of Father's anger if he found out. If he actually shot the impala, Mathew could say they had seen it near the fence and they had just scrambled underneath to get it, couldn't he?

The ground became rockier as they neared the ridge. Clumps of boulders rose between the long dry grass as they headed for the viewing hut built by his grandfather. Mathew opened the door.

'Here, Duma, here!' he called quietly. 'Inside, Duma, here girl!'

Duma obediently returned and followed Mathew into the hut. As soon as she was in, he slipped out and shut the door. If he found his impala he didn't want her frightening him off again, Duma lifted her front paws up to the viewing window and whined. Mathew poked his arm through the window and fondled her ears.

'Won't be long, Duma, girl!' he said and turned to survey the riverbank below. It looked deserted. Without rain for a few months, there was almost as much bank as water. Either side of the clearing below were tall yellow fever trees. The thorns and bush on their right extended down the slope not very far from where they stood.

'Anything?' Mathew asked Mugo. Impalas would blend easily with the shady red earth under the fever trees, but he couldn't detect any movement. He felt disappointed and irritated, especially as Mugo remained quiet. 'We'll see more if we go down a bit.'

Without waiting for a response, Mathew cut diagonally across the slope. If he couldn't see anything from halfway down, he would give up. Patches of sunlight penetrated the giant fever trees below, illuminating the yellow-green bark. The shade looked inviting and cool. Mathew looked back up the slope and stopped. If he went much further to the right, he would lose sight of the viewing hut. He became aware of the sweat between his palm and the blue steel. For the first time he began to have doubts. Perhaps his Red Ryder had made him feel braver than he was.

He was about to admit defeat and turn back when Mugo's hand touched his shoulder. He followed the line of Mugo's index finger. Good old Mugo, after all! There was his impala! It stood stock-still between two tree trunks with its head and fine horns raised in profile. Had it heard them? For it to be in range, he needed to get a little closer. He began to tiptoe forward as softly as possible, first one step, then another, his heart beating louder than his footsteps. Entering the umbrella thorn trees, he ducked the lower branches to avoid the thorns and not to rustle their long golden seedpods. Just a little further and his position would be perfect.

For a second time he silently raised his gun. He aligned the sights before slowly bringing them to bear on his target. He had to aim for the head and not tremble. His finger curled around the trigger. *Steady*, he told himself. *Steady!* He squeezed the metal. The after-shock went through his body at the same time as he heard a terrifying trumpeting and a crashing of branches. Before he could see whether he had brought down the impala, Mugo was tugging him and yelling.

'Ndovu! Ndovu!'

Elephant! Great flailing ears and a trunk raised above a massive grey head came plunging through the bush on the slope above them. Mathew felt his left arm being almost wrenched out of its socket as he stumbled behind Mugo towards the river.

The only way to go was down. They were trapped between the beast and the water. Even the lowest branches of the fever trees looked too high to climb. How safe was a tree anyway from a charging elephant? Only one tree offered any hope of escape. Its trunk was split in two with one section soaring upwards at an angle. Mugo pushed Mathew in front of him. Up, up, he signalled. Clambering on to the tree, Mathew tried to pull himself up but the gun under his right arm hampered him. He was gripping all he could with his left hand while his knees scraped along the bark.

'Haraka! Haraka!' Mugo urged him. Hurry! 'Give it!' Mugo held out his hand for the gun.

Mathew hesitated. He knew the rule even if it wasn't written down. '*You never put a gun in the hands of a servant.*' Father trusted Kamau more than any other servant but he had never asked him to hold his gun for him. '*You, and you alone, are responsible for your gun.*'

'No, I can –' He was about to say he could manage when his ears were blasted by another trumpeting. If the elephant chose, it could reach the tree within seconds. Mathew shakily passed his rifle to Mugo. Using both hands now he scrabbled upwards. He heard Mugo shuffling behind. Mugo had better not drop the gun! The elephant would crack it just by putting his foot on it. But Mathew didn't dare look back until they were high above the elephant's reach. He prayed silently. *Please God, don't let the elephant try to push the tree down or shake us off!* He had once seen an elephant demolish a tree. It had lifted it up, roots and all, just so it could eat the juiciest leaves at the top. That tree hadn't been quite as big as this one, but a maddened elephant could do almost anything.

As the branch narrowed, Mathew began to feel dizzy.

'I can't go any more!' he whimpered, although he still wasn't sure that they were high enough.

Mugo eased himself up close. The Red Ryder seemed to be safely tucked under his arm.

'Lie down.' Mugo mouthed the words. Mathew understood. Elephants couldn't see well but had brilliant hearing. Or maybe it would smell them up there! Mathew pursed his lips and cautiously lowered his head against the branch. The rough powdery bark brought a memory of hairy stubble pressed against his cheek while being carried when little on horseback. Was it Father or Kamau? Whoever it was, he had felt safe with the rough skin. It was nothing like the violent throbbing he felt now.

By twisting his neck, he could see the elephant out of the corner of his eye. It had stopped, not more than twenty paces away. Its giant crinkled ears still rippled ominously and although it had lowered its trunk, it was swinging it. For the first time he saw that the elephant was missing one tusk. Had he lost it in a fight? He prayed again. *Please, God, if you make him go away, I promise I won't disobey Father again.* How could he have been so stupid to let himself be carried away by an air rifle? What good was a .22 against an elephant? It would be like shooting at a tank with peas. '*Some idiots have more guns than sense.*' That's what Father always said. Why had he ignored all Mugo's warnings and how had they missed seeing the elephant earlier? It was his own fault for making Mugo follow him in such a wild hurry! He blushed, feeling the hot blood in his cheeks. He didn't even know if he had brought down the impala. Had he seen a swirling of horns? It could have been the impala fleeing. He didn't care any more. Even if his trophy were lying there, he would leave it. The only important thing was to fetch Duma from the viewing hut and get back home.

The elephant now stood like an armed guard, considering whether to pursue the intruders. It seemed like hours before he slowly turned and lumbered back towards the slope. Mathew felt weak with relief. He waited for Mugo to make the first move.

'He's going to eat mgunga seeds. He likes them too much,' Mugo said softly when the elephant had completely disappeared into the umbrella thorn trees. Elephants liked to shake down the yellow-brown pods for their seeds. This one must have been busy with his feast when the shot from Mathew's gun had disturbed him.

As they slithered down the fever tree, it amazed Mathew how calm Mugo was. He let Mugo lead the way, at first close to the river and as far as possible from the elephant. Mathew thought about asking Mugo for his gun but stopped himself. Maybe Mugo was letting him keep both hands free in case they needed to climb another tree in a hurry. But even when they came out from under the trees and reached the open slope, Mugo held on to the gun. If Mugo didn't hand it over when they got to the viewing hut, he would ask for it.

Mugo set a brisk pace up the slope. He constantly looked around, especially keeping watch on the thicket of thorn trees. Mugo reached the hut and released Duma just as Mathew was scrambling to the top. Duma leapt from one to the other with excitement and then, realizing that they were going home, she dashed ahead. Mugo put two fingers in his mouth and gave a low whistle. Duma returned and Mugo signalled to her to calm down. The last thing they wanted was to bring the elephant after them again.

Duma's antics distracted Mathew from asking Mugo to return his gun. Mugo was slightly ahead of him, leading the way back to the fence. It would mean calling out to him and that felt silly. His relief at seeing the farm boundary ahead couldn't take away his feeling of having been a total idiot. When they reached the fence, Mugo waited to let Mathew crawl through. Once on home soil, he scrambled upright. Thank goodness, there didn't seem to be anyone in sight.

'Here.' Mugo, still on the other side of the fence, held out Mathew's gun. His arms moved like he was cradling a baby as he passed it carefully through the barbed wire.

'Thanks. Asante. Asante sana.' Mathew grasped the gun, repeating his thanks without looking up at Mugo's face. He had made such a fool of himself and Mugo knew it. If Father found out, each would be in terrible trouble. He would only tell him that the wire was broken, nothing else. He watched Mugo slip under the fence and put on his white tunic and fez.

'It's our secret, hey?' Mathew said awkwardly.

'Ndio,' Mugo said quietly. Yes. His fez tilted with the slight nod. It was their secret.

2

Trouble

Mzee Josiah was chopping meat and didn't look up when Mugo entered the kitchen. The cook's right hand seemed joined to the knife as his fierce strokes beat the wooden board, slicing the red meat. He stood at the far end of the table that filled the centre of the kitchen. On the dresser behind the cook, next to the larder, Mugo saw the white enamel bowl filled with potatoes. Next to it was a pumpkin, a bundle of green beans and a smaller bowl with tomatoes. Mzee Josiah always laid out the vegetables for Mugo to prepare. The slim black finger on the white clock above the dresser ticked as severely as Mzee Josiah's knife rapping the board.

Mugo hesitated. To reach the dresser he would have to pass within reach of Mzee Josiah. He knew he was in trouble. Mzee Josiah had told him to be back by four and the little hand of the clock was almost halfway between the five and the six. Mzee Josiah stopped chopping. He scooped up the chunks of meat and thrust them into a black pot on the stove to his left. Quickly Mugo slipped along the other side of the table, hoping to retrieve the vegetables while Mzee Josiah was busy at the stove. But no sooner had he grasped a bowl in each hand than a cuff to the back of his head sent potatoes and tomatoes bouncing across the dresser, scattering and rolling on to the floor.

'Where have you been?' Mzee Josiah boomed.

Mugo cowered, waiting for the next blow. Instead, Mzee Josiah's hands gripped his shoulders and swivelled him around like a wrench.

'What kind of kitchen toto are you? Playing all day! Your own father didn't know where you were hiding.'

So Mzee Josiah had spoken to Baba! There was going to be trouble at home as well. Big trouble. Mathew expected him to keep everything secret, but Baba would expect the truth. Mugo squirmed as Mzee Josiah's thumbs bore into the flesh under his shoulder bones.

'What time did I tell you to come?'

'Mzee . . . the young bwana –' Mugo didn't finish. The second blow made his head feel that it might split open like the soft tomatoes at his feet.

'Is the young bwana your employer? Is it the young bwana who gives you shillings to work in his kitchen?'

'No, Mzee,' he whispered.

'So why do you tell me about the young bwana?

Eh? What must I say to the memsahib when she complains that I am late with the dinner? Eh?'

Whatever he said would be wrong. Surely Mzee Josiah must have guessed that his lateness was to do with the memsahib's son? Mugo flinched, expecting another blow. But Mzee Josiah now thrust him down on to his knees.

'Pick up those things. Look what you waste! Like you waste the time! Clean and cut them! Hurry! Mmmmhh!' Mzee Josiah breathed angrily. People said elephants had long memories if you crossed them. Mugo was sure that Mzee Josiah's would be just as long.

As he scrubbed and peeled the potatoes at the outside sink, he tried to block out Mzee Josiah's muttering inside the kitchen but he couldn't miss hearing '*Is this toto stupid?*' and '*When you work for the wazungu, you must keep their time!*' Mugo gritted his teeth. Mathew was a mzungu and he clearly hadn't bothered about this thing they called 'time'. It was too unfair! After a while, however, the cook's muttering gave way to humming and then to Mzee Josiah's favourite song.

'Onward Christian soldiers marching out to war . . .'

Mzee Josiah and his wife, Mama Mercy, were Christians. Once a week they set off in their best clothes to meet other Christians and pray in a little wooden building. They always went the long way by the road, while if they were to cut across the bush it would take half the time. Mugo's mother had joked that they liked everyone to see them in their best clothes. When he was younger, Mugo and the other children whose parents didn't go to church sometimes amused themselves by watching and passing comments on the churchgoers. That was when he had first heard this song. At the time he didn't know any English, but his older brother, Gitau, had translated for him. Gitau had also added that it was funny how Christians sang about war because his headmaster was always telling the pupils at his school that Christians loved peace.

Right now, Mugo thought that Mzee Josiah sounded much more warlike than peaceful. After preparing the vegetables he carried them back into the kitchen. Mzee Josiah's eyes scoured the bowls, checking that he had cut everything to the right size.

'Bring more wood,' Mzee Josiah ordered. 'You want my fire to die?'

Mugo hurried out again. Everything was his fault now! In the morning he had cut and stacked a pile of branches beside the stables. He had meant to bring them across to the shed outside the kitchen but the memsahib had called him to help her carry a box of books to the car. Then Mzee Josiah had given him all the knives, forks and spoons to polish and he had forgotten the wood.

The sky was now purple and getting darker. The lower slopes of the mountain, their great Kirinyaga, had completely disappeared and it seemed that clouds were thickening. Everyone was waiting for the first rains to break the dry season. The air felt heavy. As Mugo sprinted across the grass to the stables, he saw that the light was on in Mathew's room. On his return journey, with his arms piled up with wood, he walked close to the house, slowing down as he passed Mathew's window. The mzungu boy was sitting at his desk, studying a piece of paper. Thin wooden shapes were spread out in front of him. He was going to stick them together to make another aeroplane to join the others on top of his cupboard. When it was finished, he would bring it to Mugo to admire. Mugo could hear him already: '*Can you carve one like this, Mugo?*'

'Where is that wood? Where is that boy!' Mzee Josiah's questions rumbled from the kitchen door, making Mugo scurry towards the kitchen.

The bell tinkled from the dining room. Mzee Josiah strode ahead with a tray. He had learned to cook for the wazungu in their big war against Hitler and he walked like he was still in the army. Eyes down, with a small serving dish in each hand, Mugo shuffled quietly behind him. Ever since he had accidentally dropped a plate that belonged to what

Mzee Josiah called 'Memsahib's set' he was nervous. When he first came to work in the kitchen, he had admired how the same picture had been painted on so many different plates, cups and dishes and how it never washed off. Blue birds flew over twisted blue trees with feathery leaves and tall blue houses with strange curling roofs. When he had asked Mzee Josiah about the tiny blue figures crossing the little blue bridge over the river, Mzee Josiah had told him they were people in China. But when the memsahib had seen the shattered pieces at his feet on the stone floor beside the sink, she kept repeating: '*This china has come all the way from England! Do you understand, Mugo?*'

It was a terrible scolding. The memsahib had said he would lose his pay for a week. Through his tears, the broken pieces had looked as if they were drowning. But when the memsahib and Mzee Josiah left him to sweep them away, he discovered that the little bridge had survived on a wedge the shape of a spearhead. He had hidden it, and later taken it home to put in his leather bag of small treasures. That week he had no money to give his mother. He felt bad even before he had received a second scolding. His only comfort was that he had the little bridge with its tiny people from both China and England in his bag.

As they entered the dining room, Mugo was determined not to let Mathew catch his eye. The three wazungu watched in silence as Mzee Josiah set down the dishes in front of the memsahib. Mugo handed Mzee Josiah the two bowls and stepped back. Even when Mzee Josiah lifted the lids and the steam rose with mouth-watering smells, no one said a word. Mzee Josiah handed Mugo a couple of lids. Mugo suddenly felt hungry. He had not eaten anything all day. But he would have to wait until the wazungu had finished their meal and he had washed all the pots and dishes, and swept the kitchen, before Mzee Josiah would let him go home.

The memsahib was still busy serving, while Mugo and Mzee Josiah held the lids, when the bwana broke the silence.

'I am angry, Mugo.'

Mugo's fingers gripped the china.

'Your father and I have been struggling to mend the fence in the dark. The young bwana says both of you saw it was broken when you were playing. Why didn't you tell your father straight away?'

What should he say? He could feel Bwana Grayson's eyes on him. The memsahib had stopped serving. He felt everyone's eyes were on him now. He hung his head low.

'Young bwana here says he was waiting for me to come home. But you could have told your father. Kamau would have known what to do. Isn't that so?'

'Yes, bwana,' he whispered.

'Speak up, boy!'

'Yes, bwana.'

'Then why didn't you?'

Mugo bit his lip, hesitating. From the corner of his eye he saw Mathew with his arms tightly folded, eyes fixed on the table. He looked like a small animal that had smelt a trap. If he, Mugo, told the bwana and memsahib the truth, Mathew would be punished. They would take his gun away for sure.

'You have nothing to say? I thought you were more responsible. I'm very disappointed in you, Mugo. I've told your father.' The bwana turned his back on Mugo. 'I'm sorry, my dear. We can start,' he said to the memsahib.

Mzee Josiah had been standing stock-still while the bwana questioned Mugo. Now he carefully replaced the lids on the serving dishes, then led the way back to the kitchen.

Neither spoke. Mzee Josiah simply raised his eyebrows and began preparing a tray with fruit salad and a creamy white pudding. Mugo collected the dirty pots and carried them outside. His thoughts churned like the water swirling from the tap into the sink. If the bwana was disappointed in him, the memsahib would say that she couldn't trust him. She would get a new kitchen toto. He would lose his job. He would no longer have any shillings to give his mother to put in the special leather bag for school fees that she carried on a string around her neck. Maybe Baba, his father, would never be able to save enough and maybe he would never go to school after all.

There was quiet inside the kitchen. What did Mzee Josiah mean by raising his eyebrows? He was sure that Mzee Josiah would be glad to have a new kitchen toto. The ache in his stomach grew sharper. He wanted to go home to eat, but going home would mean facing his father. Mugo blinked back tears as he rubbed, scrubbed and rinsed. After he had stacked the pots neatly, he wiped his arm across his eyes and entered the kitchen to fetch a towel. Mzee Josiah was sitting on his chair beside the door to the dining room, waiting for the memsahib to tinkle the bell. Mugo wished he were invisible.

'Kitchen toto!'

Mugo winced and forced himself to look up. Mzee Josiah was holding a small plate of ugali. The maize porridge was covered with rich-smelling mince gravy.

'Eat!' said Mzee Josiah.

'Asante, Mzee.' Mugo mumbled his thanks in surprise and timidly took the plate. Mzee Josiah usually made ugali earlier in the day. He thought Mzee Josiah hadn't given him anything because he had been so late. Another punishment. But, out of the blue, the cook had softened. Mugo didn't know why and he wasn't going to ask. He hurried outside, past the sink, and sat cross-legged on the ground at the edge of the shaft of light from the kitchen door. With the fingers of his right hand, he kneaded some ugali and gravy into a small ball. He was about to slip it into his mouth when Duma appeared from the shadows, bustling up to him. Duma's nuzzling forced a tiny smile from Mugo.

'Eh, Duma,' he said, offering up his first piece of ugali. 'Good Duma. Good girl. It's OK for you, eh? You don't have to answer Baba's questions.'

3

Anxious Neighbours

After dinner, Mathew wanted to escape to his room, but his mother put her arm lightly around his shoulder. Saturday evenings were meant to be 'family time' on his weekends home from boarding school. He was expected to join his parents in the lounge where Father drank his whisky and Mother a small cup of coffee while they listened to the radio or played gramophone records. It was usually from Saturday-evening chat that he found out what had been happening while he had been away. But tonight, after the telling-off he had received from Father, he had no desire to hang around.

'Can I go to my room?' He could hear himself whine. 'I'm making a Spitfire, Mother.'

'It can wait, Mathew.'

'Can I do it in the lounge, then?'

'No, dear!' She was tuning the radio and raised her voice above the crackling. 'You'll get glue everywhere. Just come and sit with us for a while. We've hardly seen you all day.'

He stretched out on the floral carpet that was less scratchy than the zebra and lion-skin rugs, and tried to bury himself in old Superman comics. His father poured himself a drink, sank into his leather armchair and picked up his newspaper. Mathew could feel his bad mood and it put him off reading. His father's interrogation of Mugo kept slipping into his mind. Good old Mugo! He hadn't given away anything! He could have been one of those secret scouts in the war. They kept silent when caught by the Nazis, even when threatened with terrible tortures.

'Can you believe this, Mary?' his father suddenly exclaimed. 'Those Mau Mau chaps down at Nyeri have just walked scot-free! Police couldn't get a single Kikuyu to testify against them! Either too damn scared or Mau Mau themselves.'

Mathew looked up, waiting for his father to say more. When Father started talking about Mau Mau in Mathew's presence, however, his mother often changed the subject. The momentary silence was interrupted by the warble of the telephone. His mother answered.

'It's for you, Jack.' Covering the mouthpiece with her hand, she whispered, 'Major Smithers . . . he's agitated.'

Major Smithers was their elderly neighbour. He and Mathew's grandfather had both acquired five thousand acres of grassland and bush below Mount

Kenya just before the First World War broke out in Europe. They had sailed out from England on the same boat, each with a young wife and small child. Exchanging stories of the British governor selling farms at give-away prices to white settlers, they had set out to make new lives in a new country. In Nairobi, they had bought their land from the same dealer, who assured them that it was both fertile and good for cattle and there would be plenty of labour. Grandfather Grayson always complained that the dealer had made a handsome profit on the governor's give-away prices. But with rough hand-drawn maps, papers of sale, and a Swahili cook for each family, the new neighbours had set off from Nairobi into the highlands on ox carts.

With the help of the local Kikuyu people, they had made their first houses out of wattle and daub and cleared land for ploughing. When the war erupted in Europe, Smithers signed up immediately, leaving his wife and little boy, Frank, to be looked after by the cook. Grandfather Grayson would ride over on horseback at least a couple of times a week to check on them. Sometimes he took Father with him and the two little boys would play together. When Major Smithers returned from the war four years later, everyone knew his mind had been affected. He struggled to cope with the farm and continued to rely on Grandfather. He had a terrible temper and his son, Frank, left home as soon as he could to work in Nairobi. When Father took over Grandfather's farm, he inherited the difficult major as his nearest neighbour.

Father held the telephone away from his ear. The major was deaf and tended to shout. Mathew heard the voice rasp between harsh intakes of breath. The major's boss-boy, Husani, had come to tell him that someone had cut their fence. Husani had seen this on his way home to his compound. He had come back to the house to tell the major. Both Husani and Mrs Smithers were worried. Mathew's mother raised her eyebrows and sighed. It was a family joke that the major never admitted to being worried himself. Mathew waited for Father to say something about their own fence but he didn't. Instead he told the major to make sure all the house doors and windows were properly locked and to have his gun at his bedside. Father would inform the district officer and drive over first thing in the morning.

'Ring again if there are any problems,' Father said, before putting down the receiver. He looked grim.

'No point telling him that we've also had signs of interference. I'll let the DO know tonight, but he won't be able to move until the morning.' He turned sternly on Mathew. 'Now do you see?'

Mathew hung his head. His stomach was twisting.

'Perhaps you had better go to your room and get on with that model of yours,' his mother said quietly.

It was obvious Mother wanted him out of the way while Father spoke to the DO and they discussed what to do. Mathew picked up his comics and stacked them on top of the elephant-foot stool.

'I'll come to say goodnight to you later,' Mother said. She tried to smile but couldn't hide the anxiety in her eyes.

4
Warning

Mzee Josiah had insisted that Mugo complete all his tasks. His final chore for the evening had been to clean the shoes that should have been polished in the afternoon. He was tired and it had been an effort to make them shine. He was returning a pair of school shoes to the mzungu boy's bedroom when Mathew appeared in the corridor, shutting the door of the bwana's study quickly behind him. Mathew's face reddened as he thrust up two thumbs while blocking Mugo's way.

'You were ace, Mugo!' he whispered. 'At dinner, I mean.'

Mugo lowered his gaze. Whatever 'ace' was, he didn't feel it.

'You're bringing the shoes to my room, hey? I've got something for you.'

Mathew dashed ahead to the bedroom and was back at the door in a couple of seconds. He took his shoes from Mugo and held out a handful of sweets. Some were yellow, shaped like little lemons, while others had black and white stripes. Each sweet was wrapped in shiny see-through paper. Mugo hesitated. Was Mathew offering him one or the lot?

'Go on, Mugo, take them! They're from the tuck shop at school. Yellows have got lemon sherbet inside. They'll cheer you up!' Mathew thrust his hand forward and tipped the sweets into Mugo's palm. Mugo's fingers closed around them. Mathew was trying so hard that he couldn't help a brief smile.

Mugo sat close to the fire between their house and Mami's kitchen hut. There was no moon. It felt as if the great cloak of night had swept down from the peaks of Kirinyaga, wrapping their compound close to the mountain's wooded slopes and shadows. The fire crackled and thousands of insects twittered in the bush. They sounded even more frenzied than usual. The air felt thick and heavy. Perhaps tonight the rains would come. The earth was ready.

Mugo heard a hyena cry and hippos grunting in the river as he waited for Baba to finish eating. In one hand he held a small piece of wood that he had saved at the last minute from being thrust inside Mzee Josiah's stove. In his other hand he twiddled a small knife. Although he had already imagined the shape of the elephant inside the wood, he could not bring himself to start. He had wanted to go to sleep early with his younger brother and sister, so he might avoid his father's questions. But Baba had said he wanted to talk with him. It had to be about the fence.

He could feel the displeasure in Baba's tall, lean figure as he sat on the other side of the fire. His mother had served Baba quietly. Mami was usually good at soothing him, but Mugo knew that she would not be able to take away this anger tonight. He dreaded being in front of those probing eyes set deep between bristling eyebrows and sharp cheekbones. When Baba became angry, his eyes reminded Mugo of his dead grandfather. That frightened him more than anything. What he remembered most of Baba's father in his dust-filled village were the eyes that never stopped smouldering. Mugo did not want that to happen to Baba.

Mugo knew the story of his grandfather's adventuring spirit and how, when Baba was a little boy, his father had gone to Nairobi to see if the talk about the wazungu was true. His younger brothers, who had stayed behind, would take good care of his wives and children with their own. When the family heard that he was working for wazungu soldiers, they believed that he was following the words of the prophet Mugo wa Kibiru, who had seen a vision of red-skinned invaders coming with 'fire-sticks'. Their great seer's advice had been clear: '*Learn the language of these wazungu! Learn the secrets of their power! Learn how to chase them away!*'

However, while Mugo's grandfather was away, a family of wazungu had arrived in an ox cart. The mzungu man, the head of this family, had a piece of paper called 'proof'. It said that he had paid money for this land and that it now belonged to him! The brothers of Mugo's grandfather had protested that there must be a mistake. They showed the mzungu man the place where their ancestors were buried near the grove of sacred mugumo trees. This was *their* land, *their* sacred place. Their family had lived here under their mountain Kirinyaga for generation after generation. But the mzungu man insisted that the 'proof' of his ownership was on his piece of paper. He would let them stay on the land if they helped him build a house, clear away bush and work on what he called 'his farm'. Mugo's family had been stunned.

Two of the brothers had set off for Nairobi to find Mugo's grandfather. But they found that his army unit had left, taking him with it. Later, news came that a big war had started between different wazungu tribes. The British and German wazungu were fighting each other! Eventually a message had arrived from Mugo's grandfather that he was helping to carry wounded British soldiers. The wazungu officers had said that this war would not last long and he would be able to return afterwards with the money he had earned. So the family had no choice but to continue with their lives and begin to work for the new wazungu. This was how Baba first began to herd cattle for the Grayson family when he was not much higher than his mother's hip.

It turned out to be a long war for Mugo's grandfather, and when he returned home, four years later, his happiness was short. He was so upset and furious at finding that his family had been cheated of their land by the wazungu, that he immediately borrowed a cart to take them away. There was nowhere to go except to the place the wazungu called the Native Reserve. Here the earth was harder and drier. It was already teeming with people whom other wazungu settlers had chased away.

However, that was not the whole story. Mugo's grandfather decided that one of his sons should stay behind as a herd boy for the wazungu. Ngai, the Creator, had made the first man and woman high up on Kirinyaga. He had instructed them and their descendants to take care of the lovely land below. Ngai would see that the soil was returned to its rightful owners. In the meantime, this young son must take care of the ancestors' graves and keep an eye on their land. The son whom he chose for this task was Baba. His name, Kamau, meant 'quiet warrior'. The wazungu had a boy about the same age called Jack and, when the mzungu boy wasn't in school, he spent most of his time out in the bush with Baba.

That was all a long time ago. When the old mzungu died, the boy who had liked to play with Baba became the big Bwana Grayson. He put Baba in charge of the stables. He called Baba his 'chief syce' and told him to look after his best white stallion. He knew Baba's special way with animals. Whenever any animal was sick, he would ask Baba to examine it. Although the bwana relied on his Swahili foreman to manage his Kikuyu labourers, it was widely known how much Bwana Grayson trusted Baba.

After Baba finished eating, he held out his plate. Mugo took it, hoping to slip away with it.

'Mugo!' Baba's voice stopped him. His mother silently took the plate.

'Ndio, Baba!' He sighed beneath his breath as he returned to his father.

'Why did you not inform me that the fence was broken?'

'I wanted to tell you, Baba, but it was difficult.'

'What? Did you not have the tongue you are using now?'

'Ndio, Baba.'

'What, then?'

Mugo hesitated. Where should he begin?

'Must I beat the words from you?'

'It was difficult because I was with the young bwana, Baba.'

'Mmmhh! Don't tell me about the mzungu boy. He is only a child and you will soon be a young man! If you blame the child, you are not fit to be a man.'

Shame flushed through Mugo. Even if he told Baba everything that had happened, his father would still think badly of him.

'Mugo, tell your father,' his mother said softly. 'Even if you did wrong, it is better to tell the truth.'

Mugo took a deep breath.

'The mzungu boy went under the fence to the bush. I couldn't stop him. He wanted to use his new gun, Baba.'

Mugo heard his mother murmur, 'Eh, eh!' It encouraged him to continue. At least she might understand.

When he stopped speaking, there was an uneasy silence. The fire had dwindled but the insects sounded as wild as ever. Mugo felt his blood pounding. Retelling the tale made it seem even crazier than it had been at the time. It was his mother who spoke first.

'Father of Mugo, do you remember when you and the bwana were boys? Did he not want you to help him get the horns of a big buffalo?' She paused, but Baba said nothing. 'That buffalo nearly killed the two of you. This story from Mugo, it reminds me of that.'

Mugo bit his lip. It sounded as if his mother was trying to rescue him. He had even heard Baba tell the story so that other people laughed at how foolish boys could be. But Baba was not laughing now.

'That was a long time ago,' he said curtly. 'Tell me, Mugo, do you want to look after the bwana's cattle again? Do you want him to send you to the fields?'

'Hapana, Baba,' Mugo whispered, shaking his head fervently. Baba was relentless.

'Do you want to learn English in the bwana's house? Do you want to go to school?'

'Ndio, Baba.' Mugo felt tears rising. Of course he wanted these things! If he were sent to work outside, he would earn less. Mugo also knew that Baba was planning to ask the bwana to help with his school fees when his older brother, Gitau, had completed his schooling in Nyeri. Baba's wages could only pay for one of them to be in a government school that gave proper qualifications.

'Then be careful not to make the bwana mad like that again. You should know why this fence is a big thing.'

Mugo nodded. He knew very well why the

bwana had made the new fence much higher and stronger than the old one. He had been polishing the veranda and overheard the District Officer's warning to the bwana: '*These Mau Mau agitators are coming from Nairobi to turn your labourers against you. They'll be making them take their damned oath.*'

'Tell me, Mugo . . . if the bwana thinks that you wanted to help the ones who cut his fence, do you know what will happen to us?'

Baba's question struck like lightning. It hadn't even crossed his mind. The bwana might think he was with the Mau Mau!

'But, Baba!'

Baba put up his hand to silence him. Mugo wanted to explain that he knew nothing about Mau Mau or their oath except that it was a secret thing and the wazungu had made it against their law because they feared it. But Baba looked tired and waved that Mugo could go. At the very same moment, Mugo felt drops of rain on his face. Usually he relished the freshness of the first rains as they soaked his skin and the soil under his feet. Tonight, forgetting even to say goodnight, he fled inside to his straw mat and blanket.

5

A Storm Outside

Mathew curled up under his crisp cotton sheet, listening to the rain drumming on the tin roof. It was a stroke of luck. By the time Father inspected around the fence in the morning light, his and Mugo's tracks on the other side would be washed away. Father need never know of their expedition. Usually the sound of rain on the tin induced Mathew into sleep. He enjoyed feeling wrapped up securely from the elements outside. But after the telephone call from Major Smithers, he didn't feel safe at all.

He was used to hearing grown-ups talk about the Mau Mau, especially at the club. But whenever he asked where an incident had happened, he was told '*Fortunately, not here*'. It had always been somewhere else . . . like Nairobi, which they seldom visited, or Naivasha or some other place in the Rift Valley on the other side of the Aberdare Mountains.

Tonight, however, Mathew lay in bed imagining that people might actually be prowling around their farm. What a fool he had been! What if the fence had been cut by a Mau Mau gang and they had met them in the bush? That would have been even more terrifying than their encounter with One-Tusk . . . and Mugo wouldn't have been able to protect him, a white settler boy.

The rain beat down harder now, rattling the roof, as thunder rumbled in the distance. When Mathew was younger, he had often run into the stables to get out of a thunderstorm. He and Kamau would watch the heavens open, drenching the garden and the bush beyond. In Kamau's stories, Ngai the Creator rolled out thunder from the top of his mountain when he was angered. There was one story in which Elephant helped Hare to cross a river. Hare offered to hold Elephant's jar of honey while sitting on his back. By the time they reached the other side, the jar was empty. Hare was laughing but Elephant was furious at Hare's deceit and vowed revenge. Mathew could hear Kamau ending the story as if he had made it specially for him, the little master: '*You see, bwana kidogo, one day Ngai will help Elephant. That day Hare will be very sorry. Bwana kidogo, you must know that Ngai sees everything.*' Mathew coiled in his head like a snail as he remembered how it had felt to be at the mercy of One-Tusk and his anger. As the lightning cracked, splitting the night sky, he pulled his pillow over his head.

6

Strangers

Mugo woke in the middle of the night. The first thing he heard was rain rushing to the earth. He urgently needed to pee but waited to let his eyes adjust to the gloom so he wouldn't trip over his brother and sister sleeping on the floor beside him. As he tiptoed across the room, a drop of water splashed his forehead. The thatch was leaking again. He had helped Baba patch it up in the last rainy season. He skirted past the bed where Baba was snoring. His father slept lightly and Mugo hoped the rain would cover the sound of him tugging the metal bolt on the door. Then he opened the creaking wood just enough to squeeze out. He eased it shut behind him.

Sheets of water pitched down from the edge of the thatch. The rain was driving a stream across the compound and he decided against trying to reach the toilet area. Instead, hugging the wall, he hurried to the back of the house to relieve himself there. He took his time, enjoying the freshness of the air and the damp earth. The rain was a blessing. With luck it would help everyone forget the incident of the fence.

He was feeling his way back when he realized that he was not alone in the compound. He pressed his back against the wall, his heart thumping. Three shadows were slicing through the torrential rain, aiming for the room where his parents were sleeping. They were almost close enough to touch with a long stick! The one in front was bent double, carrying something. A gun? The door was unbolted and they could go straight in! There was no chance of Mugo getting back inside in time to lock it.

His instinct told him to hide. Could he conceal himself between the maize stalks in the shamba? But he needed to know what was happening. Diving through the rain, he reached the entrance to the shamba and, trembling, felt his way along its thorny hedge until he thought he was in line with the front of the house. He scratched his fingers trying to feel for an opening through which he could peer. The downpour was easing slightly and he could just make out a shape standing outside like a guard. Then Baba's and Mami's shapes came stumbling through the door. They were probably still half asleep. There was no screaming or shouting but Mami huddled close to his father. Where were his little brother and sister? Had his parents been forced out of bed so quietly that the little ones were still sleeping?

More shadows emerged and there was talking. Mugo strained to hear. One of the strangers was much shorter than the others and his high-pitched voice carried through the rain.

'Where is the kitchen toto?'

'. . . not here . . . sometimes he sleeps there . . . kitchen . . . Mzungu keeps him late . . .' Baba's bass voice was more difficult to follow but Mugo also saw him wave his arm towards the bwana's house.

'If you lie, you will pay.' The words flew sharp as arrows.

Mugo's mouth felt dry. How did these young men know about him? If they had an informant, they would soon know Baba was lying. He had only once slept in the shed by the kitchen.

'Why should I lie?' Baba sounded composed. 'Are we not coming with you without trouble?'

'Must I look, Captain?' The shape of the guard stepped away from the door.

'Hapana. No, we go.' It was the same rapid, higher voice that had asked about the kitchen toto. He was the one with the gun and clearly the leader. Mugo was surprised how short he was, probably not much taller than himself. Mugo made out a peaked cap but could see nothing of the face underneath.

With Mami and Baba between them, the young men headed briskly towards the row of banana trees that separated Mugo's compound from Mzee Josiah's. Mugo was torn. Shouldn't he go back to his brother and sister? That's what his parents would want him to do. But he also had to know where the strangers were taking them! He would lose them in the rain-filled night if he didn't follow instantly.

The shamba extended almost to the banana trees but the thorn hedge was so thickly planted that it would be difficult to get out at that end. He was obliged to hurry back to the shamba's entrance and, by the time he was running softly on the other side, he had lost the figures in the thick wet darkness. Mugo imagined, however, that they might be heading for Mzee Josiah's door. In daylight you could see it from the banana trees, but as he emerged through the web of dripping leaves, he realized he would have to sneak up closer to see anything.

Mzee Josiah and his wife lived on their own. Their children were all grown up, working in Nairobi and Nyeri as clerks and teachers, for more money than their parents could ever earn. Halfway between the banana trees and the house was a fat mango tree. Mzee Josiah claimed his mangoes were juicier than any in the memsahib's orchard and that his cook's nose could sniff out any young thieves. When ripe, the sweet golden finger-licking smell of the fruit was a great temptation. Occasionally, made bold by friends, Mugo risked capturing a couple of mangoes. With his blood pulsing just as strongly now, he trod softly towards the tree. Tonight the rain was his friend, covering his sounds. But as he slid between the mesh of mango branches and leaves, he felt a thousand fingers circling his neck. Seconds later, he heard a shout, a scream, then scuffling and muffled shrieks. Even the gun hadn't made Mzee Josiah and Mama Mercy come as quietly as Baba and Mami.

'Stop their mouths!' It was the captain again. 'Haraka! Hurry! These ones will make us late!'

Late for what? No one said it, but it was understood. Mugo's hammering heart knew . . . just as it knew why they had asked for him too.

7

Spy

Mugo followed just far enough behind not to be detected. Although the young men kept away from the fence surrounding Bwana Grayson's house, he thought he heard Duma barking. He relaxed a little when they entered the grove of pepper trees. It was the daily route he took when Mzee Josiah sent him to collect milk from the dairy. Even in the soaking darkness the path felt familiar. He felt a special attachment to this grove. His own grandfather had planted these pepper seedlings before setting off with the wazungu for their war. But, as Baba said, he had never had the pleasure of harvesting them.

On the other side of the pepper trees, the path sloped down into a grassy plain. To the east were rows of Bwana Grayson's cramped labour lines that housed his many labourers. The dairy lay to the north-west, further into the plain. Mugo waited at the top of the slope until he thought the others had reached the bottom. The last thing he wanted was to slip on the wet earth and slide on top of them.

He was about to descend when a bolt of lightning lit up the sky and the land below. His eyes were drawn to movement on the plain in front of him. A throng of people were heading from the labour lines towards the dairy! They were almost there. It was as he thought. Everyone who worked for Bwana Grayson was being collected in one place.

A great burst of thunder exploded overhead. Mugo retreated a few paces from the open slope. Shouldn't he go back home now? The lightning might have woken up his brother and sister. They would be crying. But the brief vision of everyone running towards the dairy blazed in his mind. He stood dripping, shivering and wondering what to do when lightning struck again. The plain ahead of him was now empty of people. Mugo's legs made his decision for him.

Scrambling down the slope, then half-walking, half-running through the long grass, he trusted his knowledge of the path to keep him from tripping. It wasn't enough to know where his parents and the others had been taken. He had to know what they were actually doing! It was only Mzee Josiah and his wife whom he had seen resisting the strangers. Hadn't Baba said '*Are we not coming with you without trouble?*'? Perhaps they were not such strangers after all. He had to find out.

*

The first thing Mugo heard as he approached the back of the dairy was the mooing and shuffling of the cows in the boma opposite the long shed where the cows were milked. Wamai, the old dairyman, must have left them there, against the bwana's instructions. Mugo had heard the bwana telling the new Swahili foreman to keep an eye on Wamai. '*I don't want any of my cows struck by lightning! If there's a thunderstorm, you make sure Wamai takes them into the milking shed.*' But with Juma away visiting his sick mother, there was no one to check and no one else would inform the bwana.

The milking shed was surrounded by its own high barbed-wire fence. Stories of settlers' cattle being mysteriously slaughtered in the night had made Bwana Grayson recently replace the old fence here too. Mugo dropped behind a bush as he figured a way of getting through it. First, he must find where the guards were. There was surely more than one. Creeping low, he circled through the long grass round to the front. To his amazement, he could see no one at the gate! Instead there was a cluster of men at the entrance to the milking shed, next to Wamai the dairyman's hut. With the rain pelting down, they were more sheltered there. In the weak light coming through the door of Wamai's hut, Mugo caught the glint of long steel blades. The men carried pangas and it seemed that they were making an archway of what looked like banana leaves and maize stalks. He hoped that this was the only reason they had brought their pangas here in the middle of the night. Did he dare to sneak through the gate while they were busy? If he were spotted, they would surely chase him!

Once again, his legs seemed to decide for him. He found himself dashing for the gate and from there to the back of the milking shed and around the corner. Breathing heavily, he was relieved to see a few small bushes. If a guard came to the back, the bushes would make it a little more difficult to see him. Finding a slit between the wooden stakes of the shed wall, he put his eye to it. A dim light came from a hurricane lamp up at the front and, at first, all he could see was a mass of shadowy people with their backs to him. He tried to scan individual shapes, searching for his parents, but it was impossible.

Peering through one slit after another as he edged along the wall, he at last found Baba and Mami in a row near the front. His father had that severe expression that gave nothing away, but he saw Mami wipe her brow. He had seen her do that when she had a headache. A guard stood at the end of their line. He twirled a small club in one hand, his distrustful eyes fixed on Mzee Josiah and Mama Mercy. Old Mzee stood stiffly to attention, staring straight ahead. His face reminded Mugo of an angry carving. He didn't even seem to notice when his wife's shoulders suddenly shuddered as if ants had crawled over them. Mami placed her hand on Mama Mercy's arm. To Mugo's surprise, Mama Mercy clasped it and lifted it to her chest. As a house servant she usually kept herself apart from Mami and the other women who weeded the memsahib's garden.

Mugo began to search other faces. Many looked tense and anxious for the meeting to begin. What if the lightning had woken the bwana and he had got wind of what was happening? What if the police were already on their way with their dogs and their trucks to cart them away? But some faces showed no fear. Some younger ones looked excited, boys who were older than him and even some his own age. He felt torn. Shouldn't he just go inside and join them? Share whatever was going to happen? He wasn't a coward! Then he remembered that Baba had lied about him. The captain would find out that he hadn't been sleeping by the bwana's house. The warning to Baba had been clear: '*If you lie, you will pay.*' With the rain beating on his back, Mugo pressed his eye again to the peephole. He had to stay outside, like a spy.

The meeting began with singing. As voices mingled with the drumming of the rain, Mugo felt a deep loneliness in the words and in himself.

> *'Sorrow and trouble came*
> *Yes, sorrow and trouble.*
> *When we accepted the wazungu*
> *They stole our land.'*

Baba and Mami had lowered their heads so Mugo couldn't be sure if they were singing. But both Mzee Josiah and Mama Mercy had their eyes and mouths firmly shut. They were probably asking their Christian god to help them.

The captain appeared in the doorway. Under his peaked cap, Mugo now saw short dreadlocks and the spark in the eyes that swept across the shed. A man beside him began to call out names written on a piece of paper. As people's names were called, they stepped forward and were escorted out of the shed. Mugo felt a tightness around his chest. Were they being led through the archway into Wamai's hut? Ndio! That was where the important business would take place! It was the 'thing' that was unspoken . . . a secret except to those who were part of it . . . and the reason they were all there.

As people began returning into the shed, Mugo peered as intently as he could at their faces. He looked for some sign of difference, but at first he could find none. The tightness wrung his chest once more when he heard his parents' names.

'Kamau, son of Gitau! Njeri, wife of Kamau!'

Baba and Mami stepped forward.

'Josiah Mwangi . . . Mercy, wife of Josiah.'

Mzee Josiah and Mama Mercy did not move. The tightness squeezed up into Mugo's throat. Everyone in the shed had fallen silent. The man repeated their names, this time more harshly. Still they didn't move. The next instant, a club cracking against Mzee Josiah's shoulders sent him stumbling forward.

'Get up! Don't waste our time!'

Mama Mercy emitted screams like a tiny, frightened bird as she tried to help her husband. The guard with the club threatened to bring it down on Mzee Josiah again.

'We – can't – take – this oath!' Mzee Josiah stuttered. 'We are Chris–'

The club swung, sending him down on his knees. It rose to strike again. Mugo gasped. Baba had grabbed it, forcing it to judder in mid-air!

'These are old people!' Baba appealed to the captain. 'It is not right to beat them!'

The captain's head barely reached Baba's chest and he tilted back his cap to gaze up at Mugo's father. Although he was much younger, Mugo could tell that he did not like Baba's rebuke.

'When the wazungu settlers stole our land, did they care about our old people?' The captain spoke loudly enough to address the whole room. 'The mzungu that you call 'bwana' will never leave unless we speak with one voice. It doesn't matter if you are young or old. It is your duty to take this oath for *ithaka na wiyathi* . . . our land and our freedom. If you refuse, it means you want to help the wazungu settlers. It means you are also our enemy.'

Without waiting for a response, he signalled to the guards clustered at the door. They swooped and lifted Mzee Josiah like a sack. Mugo could no longer see his parents with so many young men circling them. But Mama Mercy's protests punctured the air. They echoed in Mugo's ears long after he imagined her being dragged away.

When they reappeared, there were no clues in Baba's and Mami's faces as to what had happened in Wamai's hut. Mugo knew he would never be able to ask. Mzee Josiah returned limping, his face like stone. He held his wife by the hand, her silent face crumpled and bewildered. But as more people were taken out and came back, the atmosphere in the shed seemed to liven. It seemed to Mugo that some stepped back inside taller and with their eyes alight.

The rain eased and a cold wind set in. Mugo knew he should set off home before the meeting ended. When it seemed that everyone had returned from Wamai's hut, he told himself it was time. But the captain now introduced the oath administrator who had travelled with his assistant all the way from Nairobi. He wore a blanket over his European shirt and trousers and spoke so passionately that Mugo was captivated.

'The mzungu is our enemy!' he declared bluntly. 'He has stolen our land and it must be returned to us. That is why we must act like one man with one mind. That is why every Kikuyu must take the Oath of Unity.'

Mugo had never heard anyone talk like this, using such stirring words in openly accusing the wazungu. He could never imagine this man saying 'Yes, bwana' and 'No, bwana' to Bwana Grayson! But the oath administrator had not finished.

'You are now joined with that "Mau Mau" that the government has banned. Never reveal this secret to any non-member! If you do, the government will throw you into their prisons. We will also kill you for breaking your oath. We have our people everywhere.'

Mugo felt the quivers enter him. What would be the punishment for a spy? He had to get away! But the administrator's assistant had begun to teach some old Kikuyu greetings and a special handshake by which members could recognize each other. If anyone was sent on a mission to someone they didn't know, these signs could be used, he said. Once again, Mugo was mesmerized.

It was only when he saw the administrator looking

at his watch, that he pulled himself away from the peephole and hurriedly crept along the wall the way he had come. But when he reached the corner, to his horror, he saw a figure at the gate. Wamai! How was he going to get out? Could he crawl under the fence? The strands of barbed wire would surely be too close to the ground. He remembered Mathew scrambling under the other broken fence a few hours ago. He had been cross at the foolishness of the mzungu boy. But was he not even more foolish? He could hear Baba saying that only a fool pokes his head into the fire to discover what makes it burn.

He wondered if he should risk trying to slip in with the others when they came out of the shed. Someone would surely notice and take him to the captain! He had just decided to go back into hiding behind the shed until everyone had gone, when the figure at the gate turned and saw him. Mugo froze.

'Eh! What are you doing?' Wamai fiercely signalled Mugo to come to him.

Mugo approached the dairyman, inhaling deeply to steel himself against trembling. He held out his hand and greeted the old man with the handshake he had just seen demonstrated through the peephole. Wamai returned the greeting.

'So it's you, Mugo! Why are you outside when everyone is inside?' Mugo felt the dairyman's watery eyes trying to penetrate him.

'I am on a mission, Mzee Wamai,' Mugo whispered. 'The others will follow.'

'I see,' said Wamai. 'You had better hurry, then.'

'Goodnight, Mzee,' said Mugo. He ran off as if the wind were chasing him. He had tricked the old dairyman into believing that he was a new 'member'. It was the only way out. Mugo didn't stop running until he reached the slope beneath the pepper trees. He glanced up towards Kirinyaga. The clouds were clearing and a few stars sparkled above. As he scrambled up the muddy slope towards his grandfather's grove, he heard the first cocks crowing.

8

A Game of Mau Mau

'I'm the oldest, so I'll be the general. Mathew can be my adjutant.'

Lance Smithers surveyed the cluster of children on the freshly mown lawn outside the lounge at the club. Mathew pushed his hands deeper in his pockets and pulled back his shoulders. He had already discovered that Lance, who was only a few months older, always liked to be in charge.

Lance's family had been occasional visitors to the club while his grandfather, Major Smithers, was alive. When the major had recently died of a heart attack, Lance's father, Frank, had been worried about his elderly mother living on her own. Mau Mau attacks on isolated farms were becoming more frequent. Yet, according to Mathew's mother, the major's widow had refused to leave the farm, point-blank. She insisted her servants were loyal and that she could still handle her .22. In the end, Frank Smithers had left his office job in Nairobi and brought his family up to the highlands to manage the farm himself. They had arrived at the end of October, on the weekend after the governor had declared a State of Emergency. Rumour was that the old lady was secretly delighted. Lance's father had volunteered for the local Kenya Police Reserve and her conversations were full of references to 'my inspector son'.

While his parents were relieved, Mathew had also been pleased. When Lance arrived at his boarding school, he had felt secretly flattered when the new boy announced to everyone that he was Mathew's neighbour and friend. Matron had put Lance into his dormitory and told Mathew to look after him. It didn't take Lance long to get the hang of most things about the school and to gather a whole collection of friends. Lance had reserved, however, a special place for Mathew. His 'adjutant'.

'We're going to hunt Mau Mau!' Lance commanded, sweeping his eyes across the group on the lawn up towards the mountain. The other children were all younger. Some of them wriggled and made scared faces.

'I don't want to play that!' someone whined.

'It's only a game! Mathew and I are the search party.' Lance nodded briskly at Mathew. Then he signalled a stubby boy who was in the year below them at school.

'John will be our guard at number-three tennis

court.' Lance pointed to the children's court, beyond the enclosure for the swimming pool. John's cheeks puffed out in a grin.

'The rest of you are Mau Mau, so you can hide wherever you like in the grounds. No one goes inside the club house. We'll count to a hundred. If we catch you, we put you in detention in the tennis court, where John guards you. We've got twenty minutes to catch you all, so start running NOW!'

Squealing and screaming, the younger ones ran off. *Amazing,* thought Mathew, *how they all obeyed! Lance just said what he wanted and that was that!*

'Right turn! Adjutant! Start counting!'

Mathew turned his face towards the wall near the French windows leading into the lounge. He scanned the grown-ups at the bar and in armchairs around coffee tables. Mother said that seeing so many men in the Police Reserve's khaki uniform reminded her of wartime. His parents were sitting with Lance's parents not far from the French windows. Both fathers' revolvers lay out of their holsters on the coffee table.

'One, two, three . . .' he began loudly but quickly lowered his voice. The two fathers were arguing! Lance's father sounded tetchy.

'I grant you know a damn side more about farming than I do, Jack —'

'I also understand my labour!' Father interrupted

irritably. 'I speak their language! I grew up with some of them!'

'If you believe that means you know them, you kid yourself! These Mau Mau aren't human like you and me, Jack! Look what they've just done to their own people in Nyeri! Slaughtering their own elders, women, children! Good Christian people . . . on Christmas Eve to boot!'

'I'm not talking about those damn murdering Mau Mau but – my – own – labour!' Mathew could hear Father struggling to be patient. 'I know them individually. I know their families. I even help some of them with school fees, damn it!'

'That doesn't mean a thing.'

'Take my syce, Kamau. I've known him nearly all my life and he has – never once – given me cause to distrust him. I provide his family with work! I have his boy in my kitchen, his wife in my garden, and I'm helping see his older boy through school! So he knows on which side his bread is buttered!'

'I'm telling you, Jack, they don't see it like that.'

'If any Mau Mau terrorist had come to my farm to stir up my labour, Kamau would have told me.'

'Hmmph!' Lance's father snorted. 'My war years as an intelligence officer evidently taught me to be less trusting than you . . . It's safer that way.'

There was an awkward silence around the coffee

table. Fifty-six, fifty-seven, fifty-eight . . . Mathew continued counting but realized that he was now silently mouthing his numbers. He glanced at Lance beside him. It was obvious that he had also been listening.

'Sixty-eight, sixty-nine, seventy . . .' Mathew whispered. He heard his mother ask if anyone wanted more coffee. That was so like Mother, smoothing over any discord and keeping her voice bright.

'How is Lance settling in at school?' Mother changed the conversation.

'Quite happily, we're glad to say.' Lance's mother picked up her cue. 'We're also very grateful to Mathew. He has been so . . .' Mathew didn't hear any more because Lance began counting out loud alongside him.

'Ninety-one, ninety-two, ninety-three . . .' Together their voices blurred those inside.

'One hundred!' Lance shouted across the lawn.

Mathew turned. There were no children in sight except for John, who stood by the tennis court with arms folded, waiting for his captives.

'I'll check the cricket pavilion. You go round the guest quarters,' Lance decreed. 'Any resistance and give me a shout!' He dashed off before waiting for a reply.

Mathew smiled wryly to himself. He wasn't likely to need Lance's help. Their victims-to-be were all under nine. Since the Emergency, families from outlying farms had cut down travelling to town except for necessities. So it was a matter of luck who had called in at the club for tea or lunch. No one stayed late and few stayed overnight. It was best to be home well before dark and behind your own fence.

Mathew sprinted across the lawn towards the guest huts. Around the corner and before he had even reached the first building, he found a cluster of younger children hiding beneath a thick bougainvillea, cascading with orange-paper flowers. When he pulled out the first child, the rest meekly trooped out and followed him to their 'detention'.

'You're not much good at being Mau Mau,' he said rather crossly.

Within ten minutes, Mathew and Lance had rounded up nearly everyone. It wasn't much of a game as no one had resisted.

'When is your dad going to sign up with the Police Reserve?' Lance asked Mathew as they marched the last captive to the tennis court. In school Lance had told everyone how his father would soon be a chief inspector.

'He says he's going to . . . if things get worse.' Mathew felt embarrassed by Lance's directness.

'What's he waiting for? Dad says if we want to get rid of the Mau Mau, we have to do it ourselves.

He reckons we'll all be dead if we sit back and wait for the government to do it.'

Mathew was silent. He wanted to defend Father . . . to say that Father wasn't 'sitting back'. He had built a second security fence only a hundred yards from the house. He had it guarded night and day by tall Turkana men from the north who had nothing to do with the local Kikuyu. Father never went anywhere now without his revolver, even inside the house. He had even made Mother take lessons on how to shoot and she had her own pistol. But what if Lance's father was correct? What if Father was too trusting? Father wasn't like some farmers who had their labourers whipped. Everyone knew how Lance's grandfather used to have his foreman whip men with the stinging kiboko made from hippo hide. Father had never let that happen on their farm. '*It turns your labour against you.*' That's why he thought they were loyal. But how could you tell?

Mathew felt uneasy for the rest of the afternoon at the club. After Lance ordered the release of their captives from the tennis court, they all trooped into the dining room for juice, cakes and biscuits. Mathew found himself looking at waiters who were always polite and who sometimes joked and laughed with him. Was it possible that their smiles concealed other feelings? Did some of them really support the Mau Mau and hate him?

He tried to push these troubling thoughts out of his head. He wanted to talk with Father. In fact, he needed to talk with both his parents. Mother had to learn that he was old enough. She shouldn't keep trying to protect him from what she said were 'adult matters'. He wanted to tell them that he had heard the conversation with Lance's father and also what Lance had said. He resolved to do it while everything was fresh in his head. Yes, he would talk with them in the car as they drove home.

Then he remembered! How could he have forgotten? They would not be alone. This morning he had shared the back seat with Kamau and Mugo on their journey into town. Kamau had come to Father about an urgent message that his sister was sick. So Father had agreed to drop him and Mugo outside the location where his sister lived on the other side of town and then to collect them at four o'clock. Mathew had been present yesterday evening when Father had told Mother about the arrangement. Mother had raised her eyebrows and said 'I only hope he appreciates you going out of your way like this!'

'Drat!' Mathew said under his breath as he walked with his parents and Lance's family to their cars. He couldn't possibly talk with his parents in front of Kamau and Mugo. It would have to wait.

'I'll follow you,' suggested Lance's father. 'We

should keep together until we get to your place.'

It was ten miles to the Graysons' farm and a couple of miles further to the Smithers' place. Mathew watched as his father explained that the others should go ahead because he was going to collect his syce from the location. Mrs Smithers looked pityingly at Mathew's mother. Lance's father looked at his watch with an audible sigh.

'That will take you at least another half an hour. You'd better get a move on,' he said brusquely.

'Don't worry about us. We'll be fine,' said Father.

9
Brothers

Mugo stared in dismay at the high barbed-wire fence that stretched as far as he could see. The wazungu had fenced in the whole location! The place where Baba's sister lived looked as if it was now a vast prison. He wondered if there had been a fence like this around the location in Nyeri on Christmas Eve. The news had travelled fast how the elders and their families who refused to take the oath had been murdered there. He wanted to ask Baba what he thought, but it wasn't the right time.

Bwana Grayson had left them at the side of the road in sight of the closed gate. Ahead of them, two Kikuyu police guards stood vigilant and alert in white shorts and black shirts with long sleeves. Their tall red hats looked like the memsahib's plant pots turned upside down with a thick black tassel hanging from the top of each hat. Around each guard's neck hung a long white rope carrying a whistle that was secured into his belt, next to a shiny buckle. From the side of each belt hung a baton. Mugo thought how hot and uncomfortable it must be under all that uniform in the burning sun. It could make someone bad-tempered. Mugo hadn't heard anyone on Bwana Grayson's farm say a good word about these 'red hats'. He had even heard Mzee Josiah recently say, *Some of them think they are bwanas themselves.*

As they drew near, Mugo felt the intensity of their eyes. Baba greeted them both politely.

'We want to enter,' said Baba. 'This is my son and we have come to visit my sister.'

'Where are your papers?' The guard's outstretched palm shimmered with sweat.

'I did not know that I need papers to visit my sister.'

'Everyone must have papers! It's the Emergency! Have you been sleeping?' The guard was much younger than Baba and his rude tone shocked Mugo.

'My sister is sick,' Baba said quietly. 'She sent for me. That is why I am here.'

'We don't have permission to let you in without papers. You must go and get them.' The guard waved his hand, dismissing them.

Anger jumped into Mugo's throat. This red hat was talking to Baba like he was nobody. But Baba remained calm.

'Did you not see us come out from the bwana's

car? If we are coming to make trouble, will we be travelling with a mzungu?'

Mugo saw the guard glance at his companion. It was clear that they had seen Bwana Grayson and his car. Baba persisted. He told them how the bwana had specially brought them to the location and that this same bwana would return at four o'clock.

'You can ask Bwana Grayson yourself. He will tell you that we work for him. He will be upset that you did not let us in.'

Mugo saw the guards' eyes begin to waver. They would not like a problem with a bwana.

'Come with me to my sister's house,' Baba continued. 'You will see that I am telling the truth.'

Mugo marvelled at his father's assurance. Suddenly the second guard, who hadn't spoken so far, pointed to the bulge in each of Mugo's trouser pockets.

'What have you got there?'

Mugo swallowed hard. He had heard about guards who helped themselves to things they liked. He put a hand in each pocket and reluctantly pulled out two little wooden elephants. Each had outstretched ears and a raised trunk as if ready to charge.

'Where did you get these?' The man's eyes narrowed.

'They are mine.'

'They are very well made. Perhaps you stole them?'

'I made them myself!' Mugo heard his voice rise. 'They are for –'

Baba cut him short. 'My son is good at carving. When the bwana comes you can ask him.'

The reminder about Bwana Grayson worked. With an abrupt wave, the second guard signalled to the first to let Baba and Mugo through. Mugo slipped the elephants back into his pockets. Baba's smartness had got them on their way.

A few days earlier Baba had received a message that his sister was ill and she wanted him to come. But when Baba had asked for a day off work, Bwana Grayson said he must wait until Saturday. The bwana had added that he would be driving into town himself and would give Baba a lift. There had been no choice . . . and the lift certainly saved hours of walking. Mugo had begged Baba to ask the bwana to let him come too. He had been dying to give the newly carved elephants to his brother Gitau and his cousin Karanja. These days Gitau rarely came home when not at school. He preferred to stay with Baba's sister in the location and to earn a little money by working for one of the Asian shopkeepers in town. He had not even come home over Christmas. Mami had especially missed him and given Mugo a message. *'Tell your brother I hope he is well. He must come before he goes back to school. I am waiting for him.*' Mugo was also longing to see his brother although he knew that Gitau might be out working. If so, he would ask his cousin Karanja to pass on his present and the message.

Mugo followed Baba through the maze of narrow alleys between the cramped mud and wooden houses. There was always much to see here. Some people sat outside their doorways, making sandals from old tyres, belts and bags from leather, baskets from reeds, boxes and buckets from tin, and items Mugo had never seen before. In almost every alley, someone stocked a few shelves of tinned food, oil, maize meal and sugar while someone else would spread out a few vegetables or pieces of meat to sell. Even the prison fence had not stopped the bustle of activity.

Karanja greeted them solemnly at the door. He was only a little older than Mugo and in the past had always given him a special greeting. Today, there was not even a quick grin or a wink as he led them to the small yard at the back. Mugo had expected to find Karanja's mother in bed, but she was on her knees, scrubbing clothes in a tin tub. She was normally a cheerful person and much livelier than Baba, her older brother. But now, when she looked up to greet them, her eyes seemed lifeless. She remained on her knees.

'What is wrong?' Baba asked. 'We heard that you were sick!'

'Ndio! My heart is very sick! I couldn't tell you in the message, brother. The wazungu have taken Karanja's father. They came with so many guards. They beat him even in front of our own eyes. I asked them, "*Why? Why are you doing this?*" I begged them to stop but they pushed me –' She broke off, fighting tears.

Mugo saw Karanja's eyes become wet and angry. Karanja's father worked for the Public Works Department and, when little, Karanja used to boast that his father had built all the roads and that was why there were so many cars.

Baba helped his sister up and led her inside the house. They sat down on wooden stools, facing each other, with the two boys standing beside them.

'Where did they take him? What did they say?' Baba probed.

'They wouldn't tell us!' Karanja blurted. 'Anyone can say you are Mau Mau and those thugs take you away. But my mother has more to tell you.'

Baba's sister drew her fingers like claws down her cheeks, not looking at Baba.

'Brother . . . The police asked for my son Maina . . . and for your son Gitau.'

'What?' Baba rumbled.

'Our sons were not here so they could not take them.'

'Have you news? Where are they?' Baba demanded.

Sour air invaded Mugo's lungs.

'We think they have gone with the others, uncle.' Karanja lowered his voice as if the walls might have ears. 'It's better to join the Muhimu in the forests than to let those torturing devils take you away! People say they beat you until you confess. They can kill you even if you know nothing! It's better to fight!' Mugo had never heard Karanja talk like this before. It was as if his tongue was on fire!

'I hear what you say, Karanja. But war is not porridge. It does not feed you,' Baba said tersely. 'The way you are talking, the police will come for you next! What do they teach you in school? Use your head!'

Karanja fell silent, but Mugo saw his clenched fists. His school in the location was not like the expensive government boarding school attended by Maina and Gitau, where lessons were in English. It was run by Kikuyu people, who had built a schoolroom and who could only afford a teacher who had reached Standard Two. As well as learning to read, the children learned Kikuyu songs and customs. The government had already shut down some Kikuyu schools because it said that the children were learning to be Mau Mau.

Baba turned back to Karanja's mother. 'This is

not a good place for you, sister. It will be better for you to go to your husband's people in the village until he returns.'

'No, brother, the wazungu have forced too many people to the village. How shall we eat there? Here I can earn a few shillings in town.' She was reviving. 'Karanja will also find work and –'

'Let the boys get us something while we talk,' Baba interrupted. He drew a few coins from his pocket and handed them to Karanja. 'Take Mugo and get potatoes, cabbage and beans. I want to taste your mother's irio before we leave.' It was obvious that Baba wanted to talk to his sister in private.

Karanja complained the moment they were outside in the alley. 'Your father treats me like a child. Doesn't he know things are changing? If he's not careful, he'll get a pain in his back!'

'What kind of pain?' asked Mugo, although he knew exactly what Karanja meant.

'That bwana of yours keeps you stupid, doesn't he?' Karanja jibed. 'Did the Muhimu not visit you?'

'Ndio! They visited some time ago but we haven't seen them again.' Mugo hoped Karanja wouldn't question him further. He felt sure that Karanja must have taken the Muhimu oath. It would be too embarrassing to confess his own story.

'How do you know they haven't returned?' Karanja challenged. 'They have their eyes everywhere. As I said, your father should watch what he says.'

At once Mugo felt defensive. Karanja was going too far.

'Don't get the wrong idea, Karanja. Baba wants us to have our land and our freedom from the wazungu, just like the Muhimu!'

'Then he should not say to me "War is not porridge." Does he not know that we are at war? If someone doesn't want to fight for our *ithaka na wiyathi*, is that person not a traitor?'

Mugo felt his stomach turn. How could Karanja, or anyone, think Baba was a traitor? After what was done to the elders in Nyeri, everyone knew what happened to traitors. In the few months since they had last met, Karanja had changed. The way he was talking, it was hard to think of him as the joking boy with whom he used to tease the neighbour's goats, chase chickens and run behind the older boys. They were passing a house with a tray of raw goat's meat with its stomach and a cluster of intestines on a chair by the door when he felt acid promptly rise in his gullet as if he was going to be sick. He turned and fled back the way they had come.

The retching started before he could reach the house and he was forced to kneel over an open drain. He was relieved that no one saw him apart from a couple of small children who were poking sticks into the dirty water. Mugo returned to the house feeling weak and rather foolish. He explained that he had left Karanja when he felt the sickness coming on. He said nothing about their argument. His aunt gave him a drink that she said would settle his stomach and made him lie down on Karanja's mat. He couldn't hear what she and Baba were talking about. But his mind raced from scenes of Karanja's father being seized by police to Gitau and Maina hiding deep in a forest on Kirinyaga. The drink must have put him to sleep because Baba had to wake him up to tell him it was time to leave. Karanja was back, but the only words Mugo exchanged with him were to say goodbye. The two elephants remained in his pockets.

As Mugo walked with Baba once again through the alleys, he tried to forget his nausea and pick out the good smells. He had just detected the aroma of roasted corn, when someone stepped close beside them.

'How are you, Baba? Don't stop walking. Follow me!'

Mugo's heart leapt. The voice was that of his older brother but at first glance he looked nothing like him . . . certainly not Gitau in his school uniform with blazer and tie! The figure was clad in an old British army coat and with his cap pulled down over his forehead. Before Baba could reply, they were being steered into the next alley. It happened with such speed that Mugo felt quite dizzy, until they stopped outside a small house with the door and window boarded up. The long-coated figure that was Gitau tapped softly, urgently. The door was unbolted. Once inside, it was hastily shut. The only light seeped through the narrow gap between the walls and the thatch. In the gloom, Mugo recognized the broad shoulders of Karanja's older brother.

'Are you well, uncle?' Maina greeted Baba. He wore an old khaki coat like Gitau.

'How can we be well?' Baba retorted. He breathed heavily. 'Your mother is sick with worry and here you are, hiding like thieves!'

'We are not the thieves, Baba. You forget. It is the wazungu who are the thieves and those red hats and home guards who help them are their dogs!' Gitau said steadily. He stood with his back to a door leading into a second room. Mugo wondered if there was anyone else there. Baba faced him squarely.

'Where did you learn how to lecture your elders? You think I don't know our history?'

'But what are you doing about it, Baba?'

Mugo's blood pounded. First Karanja, now Gitau! If Baba raised his hand against Gitau, as he did when he was younger, his brother would surely not stand and take it.

'Why have I been sending you to that school with wazungu teachers? Was it not to get an education so you will know what the wazungu know? Is that not why Mzee Kenyatta went to study so long in their country? Mzee knows we shall never get our land back if we do not have their knowledge!'

'What good was Mzee's knowledge when the wazungu arrested him, Baba?' Gitau asked coldly.

'You have not even finished school and you think you can fight them!' Baba blazed. His bristling eyebrows rose with scorn.

'Will Mzee's knowledge make the settler judge set him free? Even a fool knows that the wazungu won't let him go. They took our land with guns! It is time for us to take it back!' Gitau's voice had been rising but now he lowered it. 'Anyway, we have other leaders.'

'Is someone a leader who tells brother to kill brother?' Baba demanded.

For the first time Gitau looked away.

'Is it right for a Kikuyu to kill his brother? Is that unity?'

'Uncle, if a person betrays us, is that person not a traitor?' Maina asked quietly.

Mugo's mind had been twisting with all the

unanswered questions but when he heard the word 'traitor', he was seized once again with a terrible panic. He prayed there were no Muhimu listening in the next room. He was sure they wouldn't like Baba's questions. He had to stop this argument. He gripped his stomach and began to moan.

'Aahh! I feel sick again!'

'Quick! A container! Your brother was sick earlier today.'

'I need fresh air, Baba. I'll be better outside!'

Mugo turned to the door and Maina hastily unbolted it. Mugo lurched out. He threw himself against the wall and breathed deeply. Baba followed with his forehead meshed in a frown.

'Let us go or we shall be late.' Baba began walking away. He was leaving without properly saying goodbye.

Gitau came to the doorway. He took Mugo's hand and pressed it. For a moment Mugo held it tight. He wished that they could have had time together on their own . . . with no arguments and no one else listening. He had his own questions that he wanted to ask his brother. Instead, he gave his mother's message.

'Mami says she hopes you are well.' He didn't complete the second part – that Gitau should visit her before he returned to school.

'Tell Mami I hope she stays well. Go well, little brother.'

Suddenly Mugo remembered what he had in his pockets. He had nearly forgotten!

'Wait!' He pulled out the two little wooden elephants and thrust one into Gitau's hand. 'I made it for you! I'm keeping this one for myself. See, they are brothers!' He held up the charging elephant that he had made for Karanja in his palm. Clasping it in his fist, he ran to catch up with Baba.

10

A Night in the Gorge

There was tension inside the car even before Father pulled up on the dust road beside the location. After driving out of the club gates, he had commented that Lance's father was 'rather self-opinionated'. Mother had disagreed, saying that she thought his army training had made him 'a realist' and 'probably quite clear-sighted'. Mathew was sure they would have continued if he were not sitting in the back. He had thrown in that he thought Lance might be like his father but his parents had only said 'Oh' and 'Hmm'. The conversation was closed but the discordant note lingered.

Kamau and Mugo were waiting at the spot where they had left them near the location gates. Mathew shuffled along the back seat to make room. For the first time he felt slightly odd and self-conscious about sharing the seat. He grinned at Mugo, trying not to show his awkward thoughts.

'Did you have a nice time?'

'Yes,' Mugo said, but he didn't smile.

'Did your brother and your cousin like the elephants you made them?'

Mugo just nodded. He had proudly shown them to Mathew earlier but now it was marked that he didn't want to talk about them.

'How is your sister, Kamau?' Father spoke loudly above the drone of the engine.

'She is getting better, bwana.'

'So it wasn't so urgent after all, hey? You made it sound like she was at death's door!' Mathew wasn't sure whether Father was joking or accusing.

'What was wrong with her, Kamau?' asked Mother. 'Did she see a doctor?' Mother always liked to know a doctor's diagnosis.

'I don't know, memsahib. She was just sick.'

'Well, I hope her husband is taking care of her now. Men should help their wives when they are sick.'

'Yes, memsahib.'

Everyone fell quiet. There was just over an hour of daylight left. Mathew felt Father put his foot down on the accelerator as they came to the end of the tarmac. From here on the dirt road was dented with corrugations. Father's theory was that if he drove fast, the tyres skated over them. Even so, they would only reach home just before sunset. Mathew kept his eyes trained on the bush. It was a good time of day to see animals that had been resting under shade during the day and were on the move to find water.

On their journey into town, Mugo's sharp eyesight had improved Mathew's 'animal count', but now Mugo seemed tired and showed no interest. Usually Father was prepared to slow down if Mathew saw something worth checking. But when Mathew called out that he thought he had seen something with spots like a cheetah in long grass beside the road, Father didn't stop.

As the sun began to dip towards the horizon, shadows lengthened across the bush. Mathew knew the road well. They were about halfway home when the road ahead dropped down to a thickly wooded gorge with a ford for crossing at the bottom. Only very sturdy vehicles made it across in the rainy season but there was no worry about that in late December. They had just driven across the ford and were still ascending the slope on the other side, when the engine spluttered violently. They jerked to a halt.

'Damn! This is all we need!' Father cursed. He had used the Austin sedan because he had said it 'needed a spin' and Mother thought it would be more comfortable than the truck.

'Bring rocks to wedge the tyres! Hurry!' Father ordered Kamau and Mugo. He didn't want the car slipping backwards. They all climbed out.

'I knew we should have stayed with the Smithers!' Mother said fretfully. Father scanned the surface of the road behind them. They had filled up with petrol in town and there were no signs on the ground that it had been leaking. Father knelt down to search underneath the car. Mathew did the same. Nothing seemed amiss there. Next Father hoisted up the bonnet.

'Better check for a fuel blockage,' he muttered to himself. He collected a small spanner from his toolkit. Kamau and Mugo had now wedged the tyres and everyone watched Father disconnect the pipe leading from the fuel pump to the carburettor.

'Start her up!' he instructed Mother. 'Put her in neutral first.' Mother got behind the wheel. All other eyes were fixed on the end of the pipe. When fuel finally appeared, it was only a trickle.

'I was right, damn it! It's blocked!'

'How?' asked Mathew.

Father didn't answer but called to Mother to turn the engine off. He began to reconnect the pipe. Mathew felt his mother's arm around his shoulders. He leaned against her, waiting for Father's verdict. Mugo and Kamau moved away and stood silently together a short distance from the car. It seemed an age before Father straightened himself and faced them.

'Contaminated fuel at the garage or . . .' Father paused grimly and lowered his voice so only Mathew and Mother would hear, 'someone has spiked our tank!'

'What can we do?' Mother demanded. Mathew detected a note of panic.

'We have to get a lift – and the car will have to be towed. Can't fix it here. Too big a job,' said Father. His parents exchanged one of their long silent looks. Then Father signalled to Kamau.

'How long will it take you to get to Bwana Smithers' farm? We need him to come to take us home! We need him, haraka haraka!'

'It's far, bwana! I can't reach there before night.'

'Mugo runs very fast, Father! You could take a message, hey, Mugo?' Mathew willed Mugo to agree with him but Mugo remained unusually quiet.

'He can't do it, bwana kidogo!' Kamau said vehemently. 'It's too dangerous, bwana! You don't know what people you will meet on the road. At the inspector bwana's place, the guards won't know who he is. They will think he wants to trick them to open the gates and they will shoot him!'

Mathew knew from Father's silence that Kamau was right. Mathew gritted his teeth. With only half an hour of light left, it was unlikely that any other cars would come along now.

The gorge below them was already disappearing into shadows. A sudden reckless scurrying through the trees and harsh barking made Mathew freeze. A troop of baboons had discovered their presence.

Two or three swaggered boldly down the trunks of the fever trees on the other side of the road. Mathew looked up at the web of branches arching above them. They were riddled with at least twenty pairs of furry ears, close-set little eyes and long black muzzles.

'Get inside!' Father ordered. Mother swiftly shepherded Mathew and Mugo into the car. Father pulled his pistol from its holster.

'Hapana, bwana!' Kamau held up one hand to Father while scooping up a small stone with the other. He hurled it at the nearest creature. There was a yelp and it scampered off, screeching. The rest of the troop protested furiously, baring their teeth. Kamau picked up another stone and flung it. A second baboon shrieked and fled back up the tree. After Kamau hit a third, the troop retreated in a flurry of grunts, barks and screams.

Through the back window Mathew watched Father nod to Kamau. The light was rapidly fading and the two of them walked part of the way down the gorge and then up again until they reached the top of the slope. Father kept his revolver in his hand. It looked as if they were checking out the territory. Seeing Kamau with Father and the way he had chased away the baboons reassured Mathew a little that Father was right and Lance's father wrong. Kamau seemed as concerned as they were about spending the night in the gorge. If someone had put dirt in the fuel tank, it surely wasn't Kamau.

Mathew tilted his head over the front seat. Mother's small pistol lay on her lap. She had taken it out of her handbag. 'Mother, who could have done this to us? That's sabotage, isn't it?'

'Put it out of your mind, Mathew. It could have been accidental, like your father said. So we'll just pray and think positively.' Her voice was unnaturally bright. The pistol on her lap was hardly a sign that she was managing to 'think positively' herself. He wanted to pursue the conversation but a glance at Mugo's face hushed him. There was a blankness in Mugo's eyes – an invisible barrier – that he had never seen before. What was going on in his head? For the first time, it occurred to Mathew that Mugo might think differently from his father, Kamau. Mathew sat back and curled up on his side of the back seat. He closed his eyes to stop them sliding towards Mugo. When he opened them again, darkness had crept in everywhere. With it came dread of the night ahead.

Father's plan was that he would keep watch outside from where he would be better able to shoot anyone stealing up to attack the car. Everyone else, including Kamau, should remain inside. Mother told Mathew to try to sleep but he lay awake, cold and scared, listening for night sounds. Some jackal howls seemed to come closer, then thankfully faded. A high-pitched squawking made him think of a large bird, an eagle perhaps, until he remembered that cheetahs sometimes imitated birds. Maybe it was the cheetah that he had seen earlier in the bush! What if it had now come to the gorge? It could have easily travelled the distance. When a gloomy moonlight began filtering through the foliage, Mathew kept checking for Father's silhouette, terrified that at any moment Father would be fighting for his life . . . their lives. Sleep seemed impossible. From sounds inside the car, he was aware that Kamau and Mother were awake too. Only Mugo appeared to be asleep.

Eventually Father clambered into the car.

'I won't be able to pull the blasted trigger if I stay out there any longer!' He was shivering. 'Haven't been so cold since I was in the army!'

Father placed his revolver on the dashboard. Mother lit a cigarette and gave it to him. She didn't often smoke but she lit one for herself as well. Even though his parents rolled down their windows a little, Mathew's eyes began to sting. The red tips of the cigarettes glowed like desperate signals. He wanted to say that these signals might show their attackers where they were. But instead his eyes were closing and he wanted to forget everything.

Messenger

Mugo woke, shaking, in the middle of a nightmare. Men in red hats were chasing him and Baba. The two of them beat desperately on the door of a wooden house. Someone who looked like Karanja opened it, then shut it in their faces, shouting 'Traitors!'. The men in red hats were about to grab them when Mugo opened his eyes. He was hunched up in the back seat of the bwana's car with Baba gripping his arm, telling him to get up. The car was steamed up and stank of stale cigarettes. Mathew was curled up at the other end of the seat. He seemed to be still asleep. When Baba opened the door, Mugo scrambled out, gulping in the fresh morning air. It was still totally dark down in the gorge while up ahead, above the slope, the sky showed the first signs of light.

Bwana Grayson was standing beside the car, his revolver in one hand and a piece of paper in the other.

'Mugo, I want you to run to the inspector bwana

as fast as you can! Show the guards at the gate that you have this message from me. Tell them to take you to the inspector bwana straight away. If they give you any bother, tell them that I shall complain to him. Can you do this?'

Mugo hesitated, looking at his father. He had been petrified in the night that a Muhimu gang would find the car. If there were an attack, he and Baba would be caught in the middle. If the gang overpowered the bwana's family, they would probably be killed as well . . . and the danger still wasn't past.

'I told the bwana you were sick yesterday.' Baba covered Mugo's hesitation.

'I'm better, Baba.'

'Then the bwana is right. You will travel faster than me.'

Mugo held out his hand for the note. 'I can do it, bwana,' he mumbled.

'Good boy, Mugo!' The bwana sounded relieved. 'I've asked the inspector bwana to bring a span of oxen to tow the car. You must come back with him.'

Mugo slipped the paper into his pocket. His fingers touched his little elephant. He needed its courage. He was not looking forward to meeting this inspector bwana.

Mugo set himself a steady pace. As he came out at the top of the gorge, he saw the two purple peaks of Kirinyaga rising above the low-lying morning mist that covered the bush. Already the sky behind Kirinyaga was starting to change to the colour of ripe mangoes. His spirits lifted a little remembering how Mami said that the sun brings a new beginning. Last night, in the car, he had tried to block out from his mind the horrible events of the day. But they had followed him into his sleep. It was Karanja's jibes that hurt most of all. Even Gitau, while arguing with Baba, hadn't called their father a traitor! To stop his mind returning to yesterday's misery, Mugo listened to the birds waking up. He liked how they took turns with their early morning songs. The doves had started with their throaty cooing, followed by some noisy chattering hoopoes and then the mousebirds with their tiny squeaks. He had learned to know them all as a herd boy. Life had been simpler then.

A flurry in the long grass beside the road startled him. He had disturbed a bunch of guineafowl. Without breaking his rhythm, he turned his head to watch them scatter. He even smiled to himself at their alarm. But seconds later, it was his turn to feel panic. Two men stepped out of the bush on to the road ahead of him. He had seen no movement at all. They just silently appeared and stood waiting for him. Even though it was Sunday, they did not look like labourers on a day off. One of them wore a long army coat like Gitau's and the other, with his hair in short spiky dreadlocks, wore a blanket. Mugo thought he glimpsed a knife tucked into a strap underneath the blanket. There could also be a gun under the coat. He stopped a few feet away and greeted them politely, trying not to show any fear.

'Where are you going?' It sounded like a casual question from Longcoat, but Mugo knew that it wasn't.

'I'm going home.' He tried to breathe evenly. Instinct told him to say nothing about the bwana's car and the message he had to deliver.

'Where is that?' Dreadlock's eyes pierced Mugo through the shadowy dawn light. There was something about him and his husky tone that Mugo thought he recognized.

'It is Bwana Grayson's place.'

The men exchanged glances.

'Why do you call it the mzungu's place? Is it not your father's place? What's your name?' Dreadlock demanded.

'Mugo, son of Kamau.'

'Is that Kamau the one who looks after the mzungu's horses on the land stolen from his own father?'

Mugo nodded. Dreadlock knew his father! In a flash, Mugo remembered. Dreadlock was the same Muhimu guard who had wanted to search for him in their compound on the night of the oath taking! All that had changed was his hair.

'So! You are the wazungu's kitchen toto!' Dreadlock was mocking him. 'Your father told me about you.' He made it sound as if he knew Baba well.

'Why aren't you in the kitchen, making tea for the wazungu this morning?' Longcoat asked softly. 'Don't they like you to make them tea?'

Mugo swallowed. 'Ndio,' he whispered. 'I have to go.'

Longcoat's hand shot out. He caught Mugo's wrist. 'Why are you out here?'

Mugo recoiled. If he told them the truth, anything could happen. There might be other armed Muhimu in the bush. They might make him take them to the gorge. They might steal up behind Bwana Grayson . . . He smothered his line of thought.

'Tell us the truth or your father shall know that he hasn't taught you properly,' Dreadlock warned. It was a threat to Baba as well.

'I went to the location yesterday with my father . . .' Mugo struggled to stop himself shaking as he explained how they had gone to visit Baba's sister because she was sick. He said nothing about their lift in the bwana's car. Instead he spoke about how the police had seized his uncle, and how they were looking for Gitau and Maina who were escaping to the forest to become fighters. His mind was racing ahead, thinking what to say next, when Dreadlock interrupted impatiently.

'So where is your father now?'

'I was going to tell you. Those red hats are devils!' Mugo cried. He wove his story of how the police guards had realized that Baba was Gitau's father and trapped them at the location gate. When Baba tried to argue with them, they had detained him for questioning! In the end, Baba had insisted that Mugo go home without him. However, by the time he had reached the edge of town, he was worried that he wouldn't make it before sunset. So he had hidden behind a shop building to sleep, then set off early this morning.

'That is why you see me now. I am running home to tell my mother.' Mugo forced himself to look from Longcoat to Dreadlock. It felt like a herd of buffaloes were stampeding inside him.

'Let him go,' said Dreadlock. Longcoat released his wrist. Dreadlock turned to Mugo. 'I shall bring you to a meeting soon, Mugo, son of Kamau. I shall come for you myself. Be ready. You will follow your brother.'

'Ndio,' said Mugo. He knew what kind of meeting Dreadlock meant. He too should commit himself to *ithaka na wiyathi*.

'Next time don't be scared of the bush when it's dark,' said Longcoat. 'Our ancestors walked here, day and night. Only wazungu should be afraid.'

'I hear you,' said Mugo.

He said goodbye and ran for all he was worth. His hand slipped into his pocket. The note was still there and his fingers stroked the little elephant. If they had made him turn out his pockets, there would have been a very different story. By the time he dared to turn around, Dreadlock and Longcoat had disappeared. He prayed that they hadn't gone along the road towards the gorge. If they discovered the truth, he would be in deep trouble. He had to tell Baba about his lies as soon as possible. He hoped Baba would understand. But what would Gitau think, if he knew? Would he say that Mugo should have told the Muhimu about the bwana's car? The questions left him uneasy. He wanted to push them away but they lingered unhappily in a muddle of doubts and fears.

By the time Bwana Grayson's gates were in sight, sweat was trickling from his skin and his stomach ached with hunger. He hadn't eaten since he had been sick yesterday. It was still another couple of miles to the inspector bwana's gates but he had to keep going.

He had almost exhausted himself when the shrill cries of an eagle made him alert again. It arced through the sky above him, disappeared and returned. It was circling. Was it expecting something? Waiting for him to drop? The inspector bwana's metal gates glimmered in the distance. Mugo heard his own panting. He was as loud as Duma when the red setter had run herself out. The soles of his feet smacked the ground, making the dust rise as he pushed himself on in a final burst.

Two frighteningly tall figures stood rooted behind the bars of the gate ahead. Each Turkana guard, wrapped in sun-bleached cotton against night-black skin, raised his rifle. Mugo heard the shout to halt and he tried to call out that he had a message. But he had no breath left and his words came out mangled like groans. He was falling, struggling to keep upright. One hand managed to grasp the gate. With the other, he dug into his pocket and pulled out the paper. He thrust it through the bars. Strong narrow fingers brushed his palm as the note was lifted away. Mugo closed his eyes and sank to his knees.

12

Lance Has Plans

On their first evening back in school after the Christmas holidays, it was Lance who spread the story of Mathew's night stranded in a gorge. Mathew would have preferred to forget it, but Lance had already collected a cluster of boys in pyjamas around Mathew's bed in the dormitory to hear the full tale.

'My dad wanted us to travel home in convoy, didn't he, Mat?'

Mathew nodded, a little sheepish.

'Did he have a premonition?' asked one of the younger boys.

'He's not superstitious, idiot! It's army training – all that stuff he did in Abyssinia – he knows about ambushes!' Lance answered sharply. 'That's why he thought it was crazy when Mat's dad said he was off to the location – giving a lift to his labour! You tell the next bit, Mat.'

There was no stopping Lance now. Mathew felt

himself blushing and tried to keep his account as short as possible, making the most of how his father had stationed himself outside the car to protect them. But the other boys had picked up on Lance's tone.

'Is your labour Kikuyu?'

'Yes, but they weren't just anyone from the labour lines. Kamau is Father's syce and his son Mugo is our kitchen toto.'

'Weren't you scared they could be part of an ambush plot?'

'Not every Kikuyu supports the Mau Mau, you know!'

'If an attack started, they could have strangled you and your mother inside the car!'

'How could they know where our car was going to break down?' Mathew said irritably. 'Anyway, we've known them for years.'

'I think Lance's dad is right. You can't trust anyone these days,' an older boy asserted. His comment stirred up a chorus.

'How do these gangs get right into people's lounges, if someone isn't letting them in?'

'A house servant let in the gang who killed the Meiklejohns!'

'He's charged with murder like the rest of them.'

'What if the gang forced him to open up?'

'Doesn't matter because he still helped them.'

'My dad locks our servants out of the house at six o'clock.'

'Mine too!'

Lance's face said 'I told you so!'. Mathew was silent. When the flurry of voices died down, Lance continued the story. Inspector Smithers had closely questioned Mugo when he arrived with the SOS note. According to Lance, even the message might have been a 'set-up'. Lance had plainly enjoyed being part of the rescue mission. But he kept his most dramatic voice for telling how, later that day, his dad with his own team of police guards had discovered a Mau Mau hideout in the same gorge less than half a mile away. There were signs that it had been freshly used.

'Dead lucky that we didn't find you all dead, hey, Mat?'

Lance's words rang through the hushed dormitory. Mathew's tongue was about to desert him, but Matron's footsteps on the stairs and her call of 'Lights out!' saved him. Lance's audience scattered and Mathew dived between his sheets, his face smarting.

A few weeks later, after a weekend home, Lance began intimating that he knew something that would really wake Mathew up. He said things like 'If you saw what I've seen, you'd get the fright of your life . . .' and 'If your dad knew what my dad knew . . .' before adding, 'But I can't tell you, it's secret . . .' Lance's comments drifted into Mathew's head when he lay in bed at night. He began worrying about his parents on the farm. Josiah and Mugo usually didn't leave the house until eight o'clock. What if a gang killed the guards at both the outer and inner security gates? Mathew couldn't imagine Josiah willingly helping a Mau Mau gang. But what if someone got hold of Mercy and threatened to kill her if Josiah didn't open up? Mathew wasn't so sure what Josiah would do then. He was even less sure about Mugo. Since the night in the gorge, Mugo had hardly smiled. His eyes had seemed more distant. Whenever Mathew had asked if he would come out, whether it was to target bulbuls in the orchard, play cricket or even get ticks off Duma, Mugo had made an excuse even before Josiah could say anything. Mathew worried that something in Mugo had changed and he resolved to discuss it with his parents on his next visit home.

One evening, just two days before the half-term holiday, Lance was called out during prep to take a telephone call. When he returned to the form room, he passed Mathew a note.

THAT WAS MY MUM. YOU ARE COMING HOME WITH US FOR THE WEEKEND! GREAT!

Lance winked and Mathew winked back, but for the rest of prep his Latin verbs were tangled in a panic that something was wrong. Why hadn't Mother rung him herself?

His mother's phone call came when prep had ended.

'Your father and I have to go to Nairobi on Friday, so I've asked Lance's mother if they'd mind having you Friday night. She suggested that you stay the weekend. I thought you'd jump at the chance!' Mother sounded cheerful.

'Lance has already told me,' he said accusingly. 'Why are you going to Nairobi?'

His mother must have heard his agitation. 'It's nothing serious, darling! Just some legal papers to sign for your grandmother's estate in England. We'll collect you on Sunday. Your father and I are invited for lunch. You'll be having so much fun I expect you won't want to come home with us afterwards!' She laughed lightly.

Mathew wanted to say that she should have asked him first whether he wanted to spend the whole weekend with Lance. But instead he changed the subject to ask about Duma and 'any news'. All was well, said Mother, apart from an invasion of siafu ants. They had come silently in the middle of the night and demolished ten crates of newly bought chicks by morning. Mathew probed her for so many details of this massacre of the chicks that, in the end, his mother said she had to go.

Lance was so obviously pleased about the weekend that Mathew soon stopped feeling churlish. Lance said that Mathew could try out his new King 1,000-shot air rifle. If his dad wasn't on police duty, he might even take them out shooting. But there was something else that Lance was planning. He dropped hints that they were going to have an adventure at the weekend.

'I won't say what it is, Mat,' he whispered in assembly during 'All Things Bright and Beautiful'. 'But you'll remember it forever.' Mathew nudged him with his knee. Old Fowler with his black cloak and apparently telescopic glasses was scowling in their direction from the stage. Mathew opened his mouth and his lungs.

> *'The purple headed mountains,*
> *The river running by . . .'*

It was the verse he liked best. Old Fowler's eyes moved on. Lance returned Mathew's nudge. They vied with each other as to who could sing loudest.

> *'The sunset and the morning*
> *That brightens up the sky.'*

The weekend would be great after all.

13

A Secret Society

By the time they arrived at the Smithers' on Friday, it was close to sunset and there was only time for a quick run with the dogs around the strip of garden between the house and the inner security fence. Mathew held back, letting Lance run ahead in a game full of barking, shouting and jumping. He would never admit to Lance that he found the Rhodesian ridgeback and the black Dobermann intimidating. Each time he came, the dogs always sniffed him aggressively before tolerating his presence. That was how they had been trained, said Inspector Smithers. He wanted them to be fiercely protective.

At six o'clock, the servants trooped out of the house down to the first gate, where the Turkana guards let them out. When Lance's dad called the boys inside, the dogs galloped ahead of them. He locked the door then bolted it with a large iron bar that swung across the entire doorway.

Inside the dining room, the cook had laid out a

meal of cold meats, salads and a trifle for dessert. Although Mathew was ravenous, he remembered his table manners. When Mrs Smithers asked questions about school, he tried not to talk with his mouth full. Inspector Smithers seemed to half-listen. *A bit like Father*, thought Mathew. Father was always preoccupied with the farm whereas Lance's dad was probably thinking about his police work. They were still at the table when the phone rang in the hallway. Lance jumped up to get it. Seconds later he was back.

'Urgent, for you, Dad! Mr Morrison!' Lance raised his eyebrows to Mathew as Inspector Smithers rose swiftly from the table.

Mrs Smithers continued her conversation about school but she stopped mid-stream when her husband reappeared. He was brief. The Morrisons' dogs had been barking for the last ten minutes. They thought there were intruders and had rung the local police station but no one had answered. They lived about six miles away on the north-west road.

'I'll have to go. Lock up well behind me,' Lance's dad instructed as he left the room.

'Take care, dear!' Mrs Smithers called after him. Mathew thought he saw her upper lip quiver a little.

'He's going to get guns and ammo from our safe before he goes,' Lance said in a confidential tone to Mathew.

Lance helped his mother bolt the door behind his father. No one spoke for a minute. They heard the jeep rev up and listened to it rumbling while the guards opened up the first set of gates. Lance broke the silence.

'Dad will take his team, won't he, Mum?'

'He will.'

'Where are they?' Mathew was curious. As far as he knew, the nearest police post was some miles away.

'Oh, not far.' Lance glanced furtively at his mother. 'Do you want to play Monopoly?' He was changing the conversation.

Inspector Smithers had not come home by the time Lance's mother said it was time for bed. Lance's bedroom window faced the front of the house. Although Lance tried not to show it, Mathew could tell that he was anxious. At least three times while they were changing into their pyjamas, Lance lifted a corner of the curtain to check outside. After all the hints about an adventure, Mathew was surprised when Lance turned off the light, climbed on to the bunk bed above Mathew and said goodnight. They were going straight to sleep just like at school!

For a while Mathew lay awake. The rough hippo grunts sounded closer here than at home. The same river ran through both their farms. He wondered what kind of weekend he would have after all. He was already missing Duma. Would Mother have let him stay with Lance, if she knew that Inspector Smithers went out at night? Mathew couldn't imagine Father leaving him and Mother on their own.

Mathew was beginning to worry that he would never fall asleep when Lance shuffled above him.

'Are you awake, Mat?' he whispered.

'I can't sleep.'

'Me neither.' Lance slipped off the top bunk. He tiptoed across the room and Mathew heard a drawer being pulled open. It sounded as if Lance was foraging for something. A light suddenly beamed into Mathew's face. He blinked.

'You're in my power!' Lance hissed in a funny voice. He kept the torch trained on him until Mathew covered his eyes.

'Cut it out, Lance!'

'Sshh! You'll make Mum hear!' Lance held the torch down. 'Look, we might as well start what I was planning for tomorrow. As long as we're careful we can use my bedroom instead of my hideout.'

'For what?'

'A secret society.'

'How do you mean?'

'We make one. Just you and me. What do you say?'

Mathew sat up. Lance had sprung this so unexpectedly.

'What would we do?'

'Whatever we like! The chief thing is we bind each other to loyalty and secrecy. We take an oath and swear never to break it.'

Mathew pressed his fingers into his palms so intensely that they hurt. He needed to think.

'So what do you say?' Lance repeated.

'Is the oath forever?'

'Yes, that's the point.' Lance sounded so sure of himself. 'Listen, if you don't want to make a secret society with me – if it scares you stiff – I'll get someone else! I thought you'd be pleased.'

'I am! I just wanted to think about it.'

'And?'

'OK, we'll do it.' If he said anything else, Lance would say he was a sissy.

They sat on the floor in the middle of the room with a flickering candle stuck on a saucer between them. Lance held the blade of his pocket knife over the flame for a few seconds. He turned the blade from one side to the other. Then he lowered the forefinger of his other hand towards the flame. He lifted the blade and with a quick slash he sliced the skin near the top of his finger. Mathew tried not to flinch. Blood made him feel sick. The blood bubbled up and oozed from the cut. Lance kept his finger extended but turned it so that a drop splashed into the flame, which sizzled but stayed alight. Lance lifted his finger to his mouth and sucked it.

'Your turn,' he said to Mathew, holding out the knife. 'Sterilize it first in the flame.'

Mathew prayed that his hand wouldn't tremble as he held the blade above the candle. He and his finger were under Lance's microscope! If he didn't pass this test, his friendship with Lance would be over. Lance would mock him. Life at school would be impossible. He held his breath, thrust forward his other hand and, with a hasty stroke, drew the blade across the forefinger. The pain tore to his head. He clenched his teeth not to yell while he waited for the blood to trickle into the flame. Only then could he press his lips against the torn skin. Years ago, on their bush walks, Kamau had taught him that saliva helped stop infection. He raised his eyes to meet Lance's, tasting his own blood. They held each other's gaze for a few moments, each with his hand by his mouth. Lance lifted his other hand like a scout. Mathew copied him and they pressed their palms together, raised above the flame.

'Repeat after me,' said Lance. 'If I am called to help, or stand by, a member of this society . . .'

'If I am called to help, or stand by, a member of this society . . .'

'. . . at any time of day or night, I will do so, or . . .'

'. . . at any time of day or night, I will do so, or . . .'

'. . . may this oath kill me.'

Mathew's finger flew back to his mouth. When children promised 'Cross my heart and hope to die', no one really meant it. But Lance sounded deadly serious.

'. . . may this oath kill me,' he whispered, loud enough for Lance to hear.

Lance launched into a further oath. It was a pledge never to reveal the secret society to anyone on pain of death. Mathew had just pledged himself for a second time, when they heard the rumble of an approaching vehicle. Lance blew out the candle. He leapt up to sneak a look through the curtains.

'Dad's back! Get into bed! Pretend you're asleep.'

'Won't your mother be mad if there's blood on the sheets?'

'Are you still bleeding?' Lance fumbled in his drawer. Mathew felt a handkerchief shoved into his hand and wound it around his finger.

They clambered into bed. Mathew followed the sounds of the dogs barking, the engine being turned off, the door being unbolted, lowered voices, then heavy footsteps. The door opened quietly. Mathew kept his eyes shut.

'Dad? I couldn't sleep! Did you get anyone?' Lance sounded excited.

'Shh! You'll wake Mathew. I'll tell you in the morning.' The door closed.

The bed above Mathew shook as Lance pummelled his pillow.

'Why couldn't he tell me now?' Lance whispered fiercely. Mathew didn't reply. He was exhausted and ready for sleep.

At breakfast, Mrs Smithers noticed Mathew's finger. Although it was no longer bleeding, it was swollen and it hurt. She insisted on taking him to the bathroom to attend to it but when she asked how he had cut it, he said that he'd done it accidentally opening Lance's knife. Lance grinned as Mathew returned with his bandage. Lance's cut didn't look so red and angry but, even so, Mathew noticed that he kept it out of his mother's sight.

'Where's Dad?' Lance asked. 'Did he say he'll take us shooting?'

'He set off early, while you children were still asleep.'

Lance groaned. 'He promised to tell me what happened last night!'

'Nothing happened, dear. The Morrisons are fine. He's just gone to check that all is well there this morning.'

Mrs Smithers was talking like Mother when there was more to a story than she wished to reveal. Mathew was surprised that Lance didn't probe further and wondered whether it was because of the servant. He was a Kipsigi boy not much older than Mugo who came shuttling back and forth from the kitchen with their bacon and eggs, crackling hot from the cook's pan. Instead Lance asked if he could take Mathew to the dairy.

'I want to show him the new Sussex stud cow. She's massive! The stud bull is coming soon! Titanic Man for Titanic Lady!' Lance winked at Mathew.

'I'd rather you two played around the house until your father is back.'

'Nothing's going to happen to Mathew and me, Mum!' Lance objected. 'It's broad daylight! Dad would let us go! Give us a time to come back and we'll keep to it, I promise!'

'You're as bad as your father once you've got an idea.' Mrs Smithers sighed.

'It's only the dairy, Mum! You can almost see it from here since Dad cleared the bush.'

'All right, but I want you back by eleven. Is that clear?'

Mathew smiled to himself. He wasn't the only person that Lance pressured! Probably the only person to whom Lance didn't do it was his father.

Once past the guards and the gate, they raced each other to the dairy. The bush had been cut down for over a quarter of a mile to allow a clear view of anyone approaching the house. Only a few whistling thorns had somehow escaped the pangas. The dairy was situated below a short dip. Beyond the dairy, the bush had been left in its natural state. The grass was short where the cattle had grazed but there was also a stretch of thicker bush to the right where grazing was more difficult and where the grass was still longer.

The two of them had remained neck and neck but as they descended the dip, Lance took the lead. A small rucksack bobbed on his back. He began to veer away from the dairy buildings, heading along a rocky path that cut between some prickly pear bushes.

'Aren't we going to see Titanic Lady?' Mathew panted.

Lance ignored the question. He was up to something.

'Where are we going?'

'Quit worrying!' Lance called over his shoulder. 'Just follow me!'

Mathew fell silent. His heart was pumping rapidly from running. They appeared to be heading for where the bush was most dense. It occurred to him that although Lance was so confident, he had grown up mostly in Nairobi and knew much less about the bush than he did.

The grass was waist deep either side of the path

before Lance began to slow down. It was just the kind of place where you could easily be taken by surprise.

'Why are we going this way?' Mathew felt a burst of anger. 'We don't even have your gun!'

'Cool down, Mat. I couldn't ask Mum for the keys to the safe and my gun, just for going to the dairy, could I?' Lance laughed softly. 'It'll be worth it, trust me. We're nearly there!'

'Where?' Mathew hissed in frustration.

'A place you won't forget.'

Shortly afterwards, Lance crouched down and signalled Mathew to do the same.

'Keep your head down,' he commanded.

They crept forward. Every now and again, Lance raised his head a little but any time that Mathew tried to do so, Lance waved him down. At last, Lance left the path and directed Mathew to follow. They shuffled behind a bush that looked to Mathew like the small poison-arrow tree that Kamau used to warn him about. The leaves, bark and roots made both medicine and poison. Lance delved into his bag and produced a pair of binoculars.

'I'll check what we can see from here,' Lance whispered. 'Don't look yet.'

Lance pushed aside the long grass beside the poison-arrow tree and peered through the binoculars. Mathew was left to sit on his heels and listen to hundreds of cicadas piercing his ears.

Mugo once told him that the males sang to attract their mates. They sounded to Mathew like they were going mad.

He felt thoroughly fed up and was wondering what would happen if he ignored his instructions, when Lance crawled back. He held the binoculars out in his left hand but before he gave them to Mathew, he raised the palm of his right hand.

'Remember,' Lance breathed. 'Not a word.'

Mathew held up his hand and they pressed palms. Mathew slithered into position. He poked the binoculars through the grass and rested them on the bony ridges protecting his eyes. There was a round grey blur until he swivelled the knob. A high barbed-wire fence came into focus. That was nothing unusual. But above it rose a wooden watchtower. High up, two guards carried rifles in a square lookout post. A little shock rippled through him as he lowered the binoculars and focused behind the fence. It was like a picture from the war in Europe! So many people herded together behind the wire, like he'd seen in a magazine from England that his parents had bought and kept after the war ended. If the watchtower had been concrete and steel, it would look just like the one in the photo of the Nazi concentration camp. In the far distance, at the side of a low building inside the camp, he spotted a jeep.

'What's going on?' Mathew pulled himself up.

'It's dead secret,' said Lance. 'Dad's screening this lot to find who are Mau Mau. I reckon that's the Morrisons' labour down there – and their house servants.'

'Why doesn't he take them to the police station?' Mathew was confused. Inspector Smithers belonged to the Police Reserve and there was a police compound in town.

'It's better here. Dad's in charge with his own team. He gets results,' Lance said with pride.

'What does he do when he finds a Mau Mau?'

'Not one! Hundreds! Most of them are! Dad says he can tell by looking at their eyes. They get carted away to prison or government camps. Truck loads of 'em.'

'Then why is the camp secret?' Mathew persisted. 'The government must know about it if they send their trucks.'

'They don't know about it *officially* but they know they can rely on Dad to get results. You're really clueless, aren't you, Mat?' Lance rolled his eyes and shook his head.

Mathew resented Lance's tone. If he was so stupid, why had Lance made a secret pact with him? He thrust the binoculars back to Lance.

'I'm going to the dairy,' he said curtly. 'I want to see Titanic Lady.' Mathew pushed against the earth and stood up. Lance grabbed his leg and pulled him down. The binoculars fell on the ground.

'Idiot! They'll see you!'

'I don't care! Let me go!' Mathew tried to pull away, but Lance held on. They tangled as Mathew refused to give in.

'OK,' Lance gasped, releasing his grip. 'Let's get out of here. Just keep your head down! If Dad finds out we've been here, we've had it.'

Mathew scrambled on to his feet and set off, leaving Lance to pick up the binoculars and follow. He was glad that he had stood up a bit to Lance. But he kept his head down. The last thing he wanted was to be 'had' by Inspector Smithers.

14

Accusations

Not a day passed without Mugo worrying about Gitau. Had his brother and Maina reached the forest? What were they doing? How were they surviving? At first Mami had been very quiet when Baba told her what had happened. Later, when Baba expressed his anger that Gitau had '*thrown away his education*', Mugo was surprised how Mami reacted: '*Do not judge him harshly! If you walked in your son's skin, would you not feel like him?*' Their evenings, however, were now often filled with heavy silence. There was still no word of Mugo's uncle but many stories reached them of new detention camps springing up across the country. They heard about droves of Kikuyus driven out of their homes on wazungu farms and forced into the reserves. Sometimes, when he had a free hour, Mugo went down to the gate by the road. He sat beside the Turkana guards from where he sometimes saw passing trucks crammed with men, women and children. Whenever he saw a truck transporting prisoners inside a wire cage, he strained his eyes to scour the faces. But the vehicles were usually too fast, reducing everyone to an angry blur in the dust.

He began to talk to the guards. He was curious about them but because they looked so fearsome, he had to dare himself. Once he had found the courage, he discovered that they were not much older than Gitau. They spoke a little Swahili and he asked them to teach him some of their Turkana words. In turn he taught them some Kikuyu ones. Occasionally he wondered what Gitau would say, if he saw Mugo being friendly with people paid to guard the wazungu who had stolen their grandfather's land. It was all so confusing. He learned about where they lived near a great lake in the north surrounded by desert sand. For most of the year, there was no rain so their cattle were always thin. Their families were very poor and they had never been to school. They missed their homes but had come to work for the wazungu because they needed money. They had soon learned that many people hated what they did. It was lonely work.

Mugo had also begun to know loneliness. His days were spent in and around the kitchen. Mzee Josiah seemed to have become much older. He rarely spoke except to discuss the day's menu with the memsahib and to tell Mugo what needed to be done. Even when Mama Mercy came to the kitchen and began a conversation with her husband, Mzee Josiah would cut her short. Mugo wondered if they even talked at home. When he glanced at Mzee Josiah's eyes, they seemed tormented.

In the past during his 'time off', Mugo used to enjoy going to play in the labour lines or he would track his friends in the bush when they were herding cattle. But that too had changed in the last year. When he approached boys of his own age, they no longer seemed at ease with him. He suspected that they did not trust him. They must have known that he hadn't taken the oath.

Every night Mugo lay awake, unable to sleep, wondering if Dreadlock would find his way through the security fences and come for him. He had heard about the inspector uncovering a Muhimu hideout not far from where the bwana's car had broken down. As far as he knew, they hadn't caught anyone. But what if Dreadlock and Longcoat had discovered that Mugo had lied to them? They wouldn't forgive him for protecting the bwana's family. His biggest fear was that they would decide to put Baba and everyone else to the test. It was well known how a servant or a trusted worker would be used to trick a mzungu into opening the door for the Muhimu. It was said that servants had even been made to use the knives themselves. It scared him. One thing he knew for sure. Whatever oath Baba had taken, he would tell the Muhimu to kill him first rather than make him harm the bwana and his family.

When nearly three months had passed and Dreadlock still hadn't come for him, Mugo began to think that they knew the truth and that was why they weren't bothering with him. In their eyes, he was probably already a traitor. They would certainly think that if they knew that he had felt a small surge of pleasure when the memsahib told him that the young bwana was coming home soon for his 'Easter holiday'. Mugo's smile had come by itself and took him by surprise. He had even shared the news playfully with Duma, who had barked as if she understood. After his visit to the location with Baba, he had withdrawn into himself, finding excuses to stay in the kitchen rather than go outside with Mathew. But as time passed, after Mathew had returned to school, the truth was that Mugo missed him. Even if the mzungu boy was sometimes bossy and annoying, he wasn't, in himself, a bad boy. Whatever his turbulent thoughts at night, Mugo still didn't carry ill feelings towards him. However, when he heard the memsahib tell Mzee Josiah to cook for an extra person over the weekend and that this was Mathew's friend the inspector's son, Mugo felt a sharp twinge of resentment. That mzungu boy had been present when his inspector father had questioned Mugo about the note and he had accompanied them to the gorge. His blue eyes were the colour of sky but cold as the ice cubes in the memsahib's fridge. Except for their colour, they were like the eyes of a fish eagle waiting for its prey to make a mistake.

Mugo heard the car approaching but waited until he heard the bwana tooting. Duma was already jumping and wagging her tail around Mathew and the inspector's son in the driveway, when he reached the front of the house.

'Hello, Mugo!' Mathew's eyes and teeth sparkled. His 'coming home for a holiday' face was very different from his 'going away' face. Mugo responded with a little smile. There was going to be life in the house for a while. He tried not to look directly at Mathew's friend as he hurried to lift Mathew's suitcase from the car boot on to his shoulder.

'Put the other suitcase into the spare room, Mugo!'

The memsahib turned to the inspector's son and beamed. 'I hope you'll enjoy your weekend with us, Lance.'

'Thank you, Mrs Grayson. Mathew and I have great plans, haven't we, Mat?'

Mugo understood immediately who would take charge.

*

Usually on Mathew's first morning home, Mugo expected to see him after breakfast in the kitchen. Apart from coming to make 'Don't tell Josiah!' raids on the biscuit jar, he would come to nag Mzee Josiah to release Mugo early from his duties. But on Saturday morning, the kitchen remained quiet. While moving dishes back and forth from the dining room, Mugo had caught snatches of a conversation about riding and target practice. After breakfast, he was washing up outside and caught sight of Mathew and the inspector's boy running to the stables ahead of the bwana. A little later, the bwana appeared on his white stallion with the two boys following him on the grey and chestnut mares. The inspector's son was on the chestnut, Mugo's favourite.

Baba stood at the stable entrance, watching them go. His eyes appeared to be trained on the inspector's son. Suddenly he called out to the riders to stop. Mugo wished he were closer to hear what Baba was saying. He was pointing to the bit in the chestnut's mouth. The mzungu boy was pulling the bit too tightly. There had been a problem with the chestnut's mouth. But the inspector's son seemed to ignore Baba until the bwana turned around and spoke to him as well. Mugo resolved to ask Baba about the incident. His father was very protective of all the horses.

The riders came back in time for the memsahib's

morning tea. The sun was hot, and Mathew and the other boy brought his model aeroplanes and tin soldiers on to the veranda. By the time Mugo came to clear away the tea things, Mathew was so deep in a game with his friend that he didn't even seem to know that Mugo was there. Usually he liked to explain in great detail to Mugo what he was doing with his soldiers. Mugo stalled with the tray in his hand, curious to see what kind of battle had been set up with the two armies. When he realized that the inspector's son was staring at him, he jolted so abruptly that the cups and saucers rattled. As Mugo hurried away, he heard him comment to Mathew.

'You've got a cheeky one, haven't you?'

Mugo was washing vegetables for Saturday's lunch when the memsahib came to tell Mzee Josiah that he was to prepare for a large picnic on Sunday. The inspector and his wife were coming and the two families were going to drive out into the bush on the farm for the day. It was to be a shooting expedition and she hoped to bring Mzee Josiah back plenty of meat. At lunch, Mugo heard Mathew and his friend chatter about animals and guns. Even the bwana seemed cheerful. It was like there was going to be a party.

'We can't let the Emergency stop all our pleasures!' the memsahib announced as Mugo stacked up a pile of dirty plates.

'Don't worry, Mrs Grayson. We'll have my dad!' The voice of the inspector's son quavered with excitement.

The wazungu boys' target practice began later in the afternoon. Mathew had asked Mzee Josiah if Mugo could help them in setting up the targets.

'Kitchen toto must finish his work, bwana kidogo!' Mzee Josiah said, much to Mugo's relief. He didn't want to be anywhere near the inspector's boy. He felt much safer sitting on a large stone next to the shed outside the kitchen, polishing the memsahib's silver. The sound of firing and the crack of pellet against tin resounded through the air over the orchard. He remembered Gitau saying, '*Wazungu only respect those who are more powerful!*' Had his brother already been thinking then that he would fight the wazungu with their own weapons? Guns against guns?

Mugo was rubbing a knife until the silver blade glinted when he heard the noisy chattering of some go-away birds. He took no particular notice until they broke into wild, fearful screeching above the sound of a shot. Surely the wazungu boys weren't shooting at them? Every herd boy knew how go-away birds helped him by warning of predators! If you killed one it brought bad luck. Mathew should know that from Baba's stories and teaching! Mugo dropped his polishing cloth and the knife and ran. Veering around the corner of the storeroom, he saw in a glance that the inspector's son was holding the gun.

'Bwana kidogo! You mustn't kill those birds!'

The inspector's son swivelled on his heel, swinging the gun. Mugo stopped dead still. The gun pointed at him.

'Who the hell are you, telling me what to do, boy?' The icy eyes blazed.

Mugo's pulse raced. 'Please, bwana kidogo,' he turned to Mathew, 'please . . . tell your friend . . . about the bad luck . . . he must put down the gun.'

'Don't be mad, Lance! Mugo just wanted –'

But the inspector's son didn't let Mathew finish.

'Why do you let your labour get so cheeky, Mat?' He stepped forward with the gun, still pointing it at Mugo.

'Seriously, Lance, it's bad luck! Give me my gun!' Mathew pleaded.

'Don't you ever dare tell me what to do, boy!' the inspector's son rasped at Mugo. 'Do you hear that?'

'I hear you, bwana kidogo,' Mugo whispered, avoiding the mad mzungu's eyes.

'What? Speak up, boy!'

'I – hear – you – bwana – kidogo,' Mugo forced himself to speak louder. He clenched his fists to stop his trembling.

The inspector's son lowered the gun and thrust it towards Mathew.

'That's the language they understand. Do you see, Mat?'

Mugo struggled to calm his breath. He never heard Mathew's reply because at that moment Duma came haring towards the mzungu boys. Something long and feathery trailed from her mouth. She dropped it on the red earth at Mathew's feet beneath the barrel of the gun. The mouse-like body with a neat grey crest and long grey tail fell on its side. Blood spurted from its white breast while one black eye gazed directly at Mugo.

'Eh, eh!' cried Mugo. His eyes darted accusingly from the dead go-away bird to the inspector's son. He turned and ran.

15

'Only a Little Fire'

'We'll cook it!' Lance speared the dead bird with his pocket knife and lifted it. 'Each one has to eat a mouthful.'

Mathew wrinkled his nose in dismay.

'We eat bush meat. Why not bush bird, Mat? If we like it, we can eat it all.'

'You still don't understand, Lance! You're not meant to kill go-away birds!'

'Who says?'

'In Kamau's stories if somebody kills one, something bad always happens!'

'You believe such mumbo-jumbo, Mat! Anyway, a secret society needs dares.'

It was impossible to win with Lance. In one breath he insulted and maddened, in the next he excited and cajoled. Since pledging their oaths, Lance seemed to have become even more infuriating. More than once, Mathew was tempted to rebel, recalling his small act of defiance in the bush above the inspector's screening camp. Yet in school he still enjoyed other children treating him as Lance's best friend.

'We have to make a fire, Mat. Somewhere no one can see us.' Lance pulled out a box of matches from his pocket and rattled it. He had come prepared.

Mathew hesitated to suggest the narrow strip of land between the back wall of the stables and the security fence. It was his most private place, with a small den made of canes and sticks and covered with thatch, like a Kikuyu hut for storing grain. Of course Mugo had helped him. Mugo had also given him a few Kikuyu things to keep inside the hut . . . a broken bell for a bull's nose, a sisal snare, a digging stick and a ball made of banana leaves. He could imagine Lance scoffing.

'Wait here,' he told Lance. 'I'll scout ahead.'

Mathew set off with his Red Ryder on one shoulder and Duma padding loyally beside him.

'Lance is crazy, isn't he?' Mathew said in a confidential tone to Duma when they were out of Lance's hearing. 'Would you eat a go-away bird?'

The setter cocked her head up to Mathew, offering him a brief soulful glance.

'You're such a clever dog!' Mathew patted her. 'I bet you wouldn't.'

At the stables, Mathew spied Kamau and a junior syce. They appeared to be busy with the chestnut mare. He waved the all-clear. Lance sprinted across the garden and then coolly marched past the stables with the bird held up on his knife like a flag. Mathew cursed under his breath. Lance joined him at the far end of the building. Around the corner, purple bougainvillea grew along the side wall, before extending out as a hedge towards the security fence. It obscured the strip of land at the back of the stables. The entrance to Mathew's hideout was a slim gap between the bougainvillea and the fence. Duma slunk through it while Mathew stationed himself a metre in front of the gap to look around. Apart from a couple of women on their knees, with their heads down weeding the flower beds on the far side, the garden was deserted. The chairs on the veranda were empty. There was no sign of Mother or Father. Once again, he gave the all-clear. Lance slipped through the gap. As Mathew sneaked after him, he heard a whistle. Lance had spotted the den. Duma had already settled down inside its shade.

'You're a sly one, not showing me –'

'I'll get wood for the fire.' Mathew interrupted. He retreated through the bougainvillea before Lance had time to go on.

When he returned, Lance was engrossed in dissecting the bird with his knife. He had already taken off its head and tail. Mathew didn't ask if Lance had taken a peek into his den. He looked for somewhere to build the fire. The only place with dry earth and not much grass was around the den itself. He put down his armful of sticks, branches and a couple of small logs in front of it. There was barely six feet to the fence. On the other side was Father's field of dried maize.

'It's not safe, Lance! We're too near to the field,' he said nervously.

'Rubbish! You just don't want to eat this, do you?' Lance flicked the tail feathers across Mathew's nose.

'Get off!' yelled Mathew.

'Shhh! They'll hear us!' Lance chuckled. 'It's only a little fire, Mat. We'll watch over it.'

Mathew yielded. The bird was so small that it wouldn't take long to cook and they would put out the fire before they left. He wanted to show Lance how neatly he could make a fire even if he could never be as deft as Mugo. He began with a little ball of kindling twigs, then built up a tepee of sticks and a cabin of branches around the tepee. When the last pieces of wood were in place, he half expected Lance to insist on starting the fire himself. Instead Lance threw him the box of matches. Mathew lit one and slipped it through the tepee. The spark caught first time and he blew gently at the base to help the kindling. As smoke rose, he wondered about the smell. He hoped it wouldn't carry into the stables. If Kamau came to investigate, he would tell them to put it out. Lance would be difficult and Kamau would report them to Father . . . then Mathew would get the telling-off of a lifetime. Lance, however, seemed quite unworried. He produced a small ball of wire from his pocket that he unravelled and pierced through the go-away's breast. Stringing the ends of the wire around two sticks, he gave one of them to Mathew. Both had to hold the bird above the fire with its blood dripping into the flames.

The heat burned Mathew's face. If only he could think of the bird like a piece of chicken, then he would be able to fulfil the dare. After all, the herd boys caught all kinds of creatures from the bush to cook and eat. Lance was probably right. Kamau's stories and Mugo's warnings were just based on superstition. He should be more sensible.

Nevertheless, Mathew waited for Lance to take the first bite. The bird was still strung on the wire. By now its heart was surely burnt.

'It's good!' Lance licked his lips. He passed the wire to Mathew with a wide smile. Duma had come out of the den to watch and drool.

Mathew would have been all right eating his first mouthful if, at that same moment, Lance hadn't thrown the go-away's crested head into the fire. Its black eye fixed Mathew with the stare of the dead as its crested feathers sparked into flames. A wild queasiness rose up from his stomach. He spun around and spat out the thing in his mouth.

The sickness rising inside him left him dizzy.

'What's wrong, Mat? I've eaten mine. It's fine!' He vaguely heard Lance but couldn't help himself. He doubled over and was violently sick.

It was a while before he stopped shuddering. Duma came close to comfort him. Mathew avoided looking at Lance, waiting to hear his ridicule. Even worse, Lance might insist that Mathew still had to eat his share. Instead he was surprised.

'Jeez, Mat, what happened?' Lance actually sounded worried.

Mathew gestured 'I don't know'. Slowly, he made himself turn back towards the fire. To his relief and amazement, Lance had begun to throw on sand to put it out.

'I heard your mother calling us. You didn't hear her, throwing up like that!' It sounded as if Lance was turning it into a joke. 'Hurry! Give me a hand!' He threw Mathew a digging stick to loosen some soil. Mathew recognized it as the stick he kept in his den. So Lance had gone inside. But, with his stomach still feeling raw, he said nothing as he began to dig while Lance threw on a few more handfuls of sand.

'Mathew! Lance! Where are you?'

This time he heard Mother call. It sounded as if she had come into the garden to look for them. The last thing he wanted was for her to peer through the bougainvillea and see signs of a fire.

There wasn't time now to think how to cover it up completely. They just had to get Mother off their track. An idea flew into Mathew's head.

'Slip out when Mother turns her back,' he instructed Lance. 'Tell her I'm hiding but you'll find and bring me. I'll sort out the fire.'

For once, Lance didn't argue. He did what Mathew said.

There were no longer any flames but the larger pieces of wood were still burning. Mathew kept on digging and throwing on more sand. The best thing would be to bring some water to douse it and be absolutely sure. However, with Mother in the garden and Father probably sitting on the veranda with his early evening drink, he couldn't do it right away. Instead he doubled his efforts to get more sand from the hard dry earth. By the time he heard Lance whistling for him to come out, he was satisfied that he had done a good job. All that remained was a little smouldering from the largest piece of wood. That should soon die out. No red embers remained. He picked up his Red Ryder. Duma stretched and shook herself. Mathew was already feeling a little better.

'Come, Duma. Shall we see what Josiah has for us?'

Mathew was woken in the night by Father shouting. Outside the horses were whinnying frantically. He rolled out of bed in panic and fumbled across the room to his door. The corridor light was on. The front door banged and he heard the bolt being pulled across. Mother came hurrying towards him in her nightgown, pistol in one hand, pointed to the floor. Her hair was down and her eyes frightened. Her words tumbled in a fearful rush.

'Lock your windows! Don't put on the light! I'll have to wake Lance!'

But the door to the spare bedroom had already opened. Lance stood bemused in his pyjamas.

'Where's Father gone?' Mathew yelled.

'The stables! Lock up and hurry to Father's study!' Mother disappeared with Lance into the spare room.

Mathew's mind ran riot as he stumbled back across his room. Dead guards, slashed security fences, intruders in the stables attacking the horses . . . and Father single-handedly trying to confront them. If the intruders got into the house, there was only Mother and her pistol. He hoped that she had the key to Father's safe, so he could get his Red Ryder. He crouched below the window sill and thrust up a hand behind the curtains. He groped for the handle to pull the window shut. As he did so, his nose prickled. Something was burning. Looking up, he glimpsed the night sky. There was something wrong with its colour. Heart racing, he stood up and put his eye to the slit between the curtain and the window frame. A peculiar orange haze clouded the sky on his right . . . the direction of the stables.

Ignoring Mother's instructions, he dashed down the empty corridor towards the lounge. The French windows faced the stables and the maize field. He threw open the door. Even before he reached the windows, he sensed the unusual light behind the curtains. The horses' whinnying was louder than ever. He lifted a corner of the material. Scarlet flames soared above the stables. Clouds of smoke billowed upwards. Thank goodness, the wind was carrying them away from the house. Already the fire stretched as far as he could see across the maize field. Mathew's eyes veered desperately across the garden that was bathed in an eerie light. There were shadows everywhere but no obvious sign of intruders. *Where was Father?* The question hammered through his brain until there was a burst of movement from the stables. Father's stallion galloped out into the garden. Wild with terror, four other horses followed, including the grey and chestnut mares. The stallion suddenly careered away from the others, bolted past the French windows and disappeared around the front of the house. Was it hoping to get out of the gate?

Father now appeared at the entrance to the stables, silhouetted against flames. With his pistol raised, and with eyes sweeping left and right, Father also ran in the direction of the gates. Was he going to get help from the guards? Behind him, the bougainvillea bush burned brightly. The stables, the maize field and the strip of land between them, would be reduced to ashes by morning. It was like a scene from one of his war comics . . . or a nightmare. Mathew pinched his arm until it hurt. No, this was real enough. As real as the fact that he had forgotten to go back to his den and the dying fire with a jug of water. He watched, mesmerized, paralysed with fear.

'I told you to come to the study!' Mother startled him. She and Lance entered the lounge.

'Father has saved the horses, Mother!' His voice was no more than a whimper.

Lance slipped past Mathew to peep through the curtains.

'Jeez!' His face looked almost as white as Father's stallion.

'Come away from –'

A loud knocking interrupted Mother. Father's voice from outside the front door sent them all scurrying to it. Mother pulled back the bolt.

Father stepped inside, coughing. He was blackened from soot and ash.

'Oh my goodness!' Mother gasped. 'Did you see anyone?'

'No, probably far away already! Burning our

maize is one thing but setting light to my *horses* . . .' Father smouldered with rage. 'It's despicable!'

Mathew shrank to the wall. But Lance stepped up to Father.

'It's Mau Mau, isn't it, Mr Grayson?'

'Who else could it be?' Father replied.

'You should call my dad.'

16

Caged

Mugo woke with Baba shaking him, telling him to get up and come. It was the middle of the night. Immediately he thought that Dreadlock must be waiting outside. With a silent prayer that he would be brave, and that this had nothing to do with bad luck from the eye of the dead go-away bird, he followed Baba through the door. A half-moon glittered high above Kirinyaga and inspired a quick second prayer that Gitau was safe. Mugo could no longer look up at the mountain without thinking of his brother deep in its forests. At least Gitau's spirit would be with him when he took his oath for *ithaka na wiyathi*.

The compound was alive with shadows, but Mugo could see no one there. Did Baba have orders to take him to a secret meeting place? However just a few steps further on, as they turned their backs to Kirinyaga, he saw a strange orange glow in the night sky beyond the bwana's farmhouse. Fire!

'Can you hear them, Mugo? My horses . . . they are crying!'

Baba began running. Mugo had to match his long strides. His father always had a sixth sense with his animals. The wind was blowing the fire clouds away from them but even so, as they approached the security fence, Mugo felt wafts of burning air and now heard the faint cries. If there was still the old fence, they could have scrambled through and cut across the orchards straight to the stables. Instead they had to run all the way along the outside towards the gate. With every step the terrified whinnying grew louder. Was this the dead go-away bird's bad luck?

At the corner of the fence, near the front of the house, Baba's hand gripped Mugo's shoulder. Ahead of them, trees were outlined against a blaze of flames and smoke. The whole maize field was alight. Baba's fingers pressed him to slow him down. The Turkana guards at the security gates might mistake them for intruders.

Mugo walked beside Baba, warm from running but strangely cold inside. The stables were set back, blocked from view by the house. The neighing of the horses remained frenzied, mixed in with the roar and crackling of fire. When they made out the cloaks of the guards, Baba stopped and called out.

'It's me, Kamau, the one who looks after the bwana's horses.' He stretched out his arms so they could see he wasn't carrying a weapon.

'Stay there! Put up your hands!'

Mugo raised his hands even faster than Baba. He recognized the voice of the Turkana guard with whom he had exchanged some words.

'Who is that with you?'

'It is my son, the toto who works in the bwana's kitchen.'

'What do you want, Mzee?' The guard's tone seemed to soften a little.

'Somebody must free the bwana's horses! Let me in. I will do it!'

'Mzee, we can't let you in. Bwana's order.'

'Then call the bwana! He is sleeping and his horses are dying!'

'Bwana knows. He is there now.'

'Go and tell him that I am here. I have come to help him!'

'I can't do it, Mzee. Bwana says we must always be two here. We mustn't leave the gate.'

Baba wiped his face. Mugo could see that it was pointless arguing. The guards had been given their orders and were taking no chances. But just as Baba signalled to Mugo that they should go, the bwana's stallion came galloping wildly from the garden towards the gate. Its white coat, wet with sweat, was blackened with ash. It snorted and shivered, eyes and nostrils flaring. It didn't see the bwana's truck, parked on the driveway, until it was too late. It reared up on to its back legs to avoid a crash. Baba moved up to the fence.

'Jafari!' he called gently. 'Jafari! Jafari!' Baba kept repeating the stallion's name until it stood still, rooted to the ground. Baba continued murmuring and reassuring. The guards were also silent. Mugo marvelled at how the stallion seemed to understand his father. He was so absorbed in watching the two of them, that he didn't see or hear the bwana approaching.

'Kamau? Mugo?' Suspicion swelled in the bwana's voice. 'What are you doing here?'

Mugo looked up to see a pistol pointing at them. Only a few hours ago, the inspector's son had threatened to shoot him . . . and now the bwana!

'The horses, they were crying, bwana,' Baba said swiftly in defence. 'We came to help them. But the guards said we cannot come inside.'

'How did you know about the fire? It's far from your place.' The whites of the bwana's eyes gleamed against his strangely blackened face, as distrustful as his words.

'No, bwana!' Baba protested. 'You can see it in the sky, bwana.'

A wild neighing erupted from the garden.

'Give me a chance, bwana, and I will make them all quiet.'

The bwana shook his head. 'No, they'll settle down soon by themselves.'

'Bwana, we can help you stop the fire.'

'No, it's not necessary! It will burn itself out now.' The bwana spoke roughly. 'I'll see you in the morning. Go!'

A ball of anger lodged in Mugo's throat and another in his stomach as he followed Baba away. Baba had been humiliated. Neither of them spoke on the way home. They found Mami awake, waiting anxiously. She had seen the orange haze in the sky. Baba simply told her that fire had eaten up the stables but the horses were safe and the bwana didn't need their help. He said nothing about the bwana having raised his gun towards them.

It took Mugo a long time to fall asleep with a battle raging in his head. His brother would be happy to hear about the bwana losing all his maize! If the horses had been burnt alive, Gitau might even say that it was a good way to hurt the bwana because he looked after his animals better than his labourers. He could imagine Gitau saying, '*Wazungu don't care when we suffer. We are insects to them. Our father is a fool. The bwana puts a gun in his face and Baba still wants to help him!*' Yet the horses' cries had been pitiful. Mugo understood why Baba had wanted to help them. Why should any of Ngai's creatures have to suffer like that?

The police arrived before sunrise. Mugo had pulled on his white tunic and opened the door when he spotted the tall red hats coming through the trees. He yelled to Baba but his father didn't even bother to look up from washing his face. It seemed that he was already expecting them. There were six black policemen, carrying batons and two with rifles. They wanted Baba and Mugo. However, when they said they wanted Mami as well, Baba protested that there were young children at home. A red hat with a rifle said bluntly that those were their orders. The mzungu inspector was waiting at the bwana's house and they had to come without delay. If Mami couldn't leave the children, she must bring them with her. Mugo's young brother chewed on his thumb and his little sister began to howl. Mugo picked her up and she clung to him. It comforted him to hold her, if only for a few seconds. He had to hand her to Mami. He and Baba were being hurried in advance, a red hat either side, and two behind them with the guns. There was not even time to say goodbye.

Kirinyaga was shrouded in mist. Ahead of them, shouts beyond the mugumo trees and a glimpse of red between the banana bushes in Mzee Josiah's compound told Mugo that they were not the only ones. If Mzee Josiah and Mama Mercy were being rounded up, it meant that everyone was going to be questioned about the fire. But something in Baba's face, and the memory of the bwana pointing

148

his pistol at them, told him that he and Baba were getting special attention.

They were marched to the front of the house past the fence where a few hours ago Baba had calmed Jafari. Two large trucks with enormous wire cages at the back were parked outside the security fence. The smell of last night's burning sickened him. The maize field was now blackened stubble. Where yesterday there had been stables, today there was ash and rubble.

The Turkana guards opened the gates as he and Baba were marched inside to the driveway. Mugo didn't look at them. His eyes were on a police jeep with a small wire cage. The inspector stood beside it with the bwana. There was no trace of last night's wildness in the bwana. He must have washed from head to foot. He was aware of Mathew and the inspector's son with the memsahib standing on the veranda. All these wazungu were waiting for them.

'So, these are the two from last night.' The inspector's finger swung from Baba to Mugo.

'Yes. Kamau has been my stable boy and syce for years.' The bwana spoke without looking at Baba. 'He was also with us the night we were caught in the gully, remember?'

'And this is the same boy you sent to fetch me that morning?'

'Yes, Kamau's son Mugo. The younger one.'

The younger one. Mugo felt a new shock. Did they know something about Gitau?

'We'll rule nothing out. We'll get to the truth, don't worry.' The inspector signalled to the red hats to put Baba and Mugo into the jeep.

The bwana finally looked at Baba and Mugo.

'I hope the inspector finds that you two had nothing to do with this.' He turned away as the red hats pushed them roughly up into the cage.

Part of Mugo wanted to burst out shouting at the bwana to make him understand that Baba, of all people, would never have set the stables on fire. But of course that was pointless. Baba's silence began to fill him with a terrible fear.

The inspector climbed into the jeep and reversed it towards the veranda. Through the bars of the cage, Mugo saw the inspector's son smile and nudge Mathew. Mugo remembered his words after killing the go-away bird. *'Don't you ever dare tell me what to do, boy!'* But Mathew didn't raise his head towards Mugo until the jeep revved up. For a brief moment, their eyes met. Then the jeep swung forward, making him clutch the edge of the metal seat. The vehicle swept through the security gates, and bounced on to the dirt track that led past the burnt maize field to the main road. Red hats were now herding people on to the trucks with wire cages while two wazungu officers stood watching. Mugo glimpsed Mami with his brother and sister in the crowd. He opened his mouth but no sound emerged. He felt empty.

17

'I'll cut you dead forever'

Mathew felt Lance whispering into his ear but heard nothing. His head spun with jumbled pictures. It was like a nightmare in which everything happened too fast. Mugo and Kamau disappearing in a caged jeep across the burnt land. Mugo's eyes piercing him. Police yelling 'Haraka! Haraka! Hurry!', forcing people whose faces Mathew knew on to trucks, threatening them with batons and rifle butts. Children squealing with fright. Accusing stares as he, bwana kidogo, stood on the veranda. He should have walked away but he felt compelled to watch. Then his eyes fell on Mercy and Josiah. Their eyes brimmed with reproach. '*Oh, bwana kidogo, how can you do this to us?*'

It was suddenly too much. He felt drained, too tired to stand. He clutched the railing.

'Come inside, Mathew. There's no need for you to see all this.' Mother sounded far away, but he felt her arm firmly around his shoulder. 'Lance, will you help me?'

'Sure, Mrs Grayson. It must be quite a shock for Mat.'

Wedged between Mother and Lance, Mathew let himself be guided to his bedroom.

'You'll feel much better after a nap,' Mother said as he rolled over on to his bed. 'Why don't you have one too, Lance? Neither of you had enough sleep last night.'

'I'm fine thanks, Mrs Grayson. I'll watch the rest of the action, so I can tell Mat later.' Lance was as confident as ever. Even before they had left the room, Mathew had closed his eyes. For the time being, he just wanted to block everything out. It was all a mistake, spiralling out of control. But the thought of telling Father the truth petrified him. Perhaps when he woke up . . .

He had just dropped off to sleep when Lance shot back into the room, waking him.

'My dad's come back! Says once he begins screening, he won't have time to collect me. So I'm going with him now. We won't see each other until after the hols, hey?'

Mathew propped himself up, his elbow on his pillow, and managed a nod. Lance bent forward and brought his face up close. The blue web around each pupil tightened as if aiming through a gun sight.

'You split on us, Mat, and I'll cut you dead forever.'

18

Speechless

Mugo knelt on the concrete floor, gripping his hands over his ears. Baba's pain tore through him. Howls. Roars. Screams. Mugo had never heard any human being in such agony. He was alone in a small dusky room without windows and stale air next to the one in which the inspector and his men had taken Baba. They wanted him to hear. They wanted him to know that they could do anything. However hard he clenched his sweating palms over his ears, the painful sounds kept coming . . . rising and falling, rising and falling.

When they came to him, Mugo could answer none of the inspector's questions.

'Who set fire to your bwana's stables?'

'Where is your older brother?'

'When did you take the oath?'

'Did your brother give you the oath?'

'Where do you take him food?'

Each time Mugo said he didn't know – he hadn't

taken any oath and, no, he didn't do these things
– a red hat thrust his head into a bucket of freezing
water. Each time they held him down longer.
Fingers pressed on the back of his neck. A hand
shoved his scalp backwards and forwards. He was
suffocating, gulping, drowning.

19

Confession and confusion

'. . . *I'll cut you dead forever.*' Lance's threat reverberated in Mathew's head. Lance meant it. If Mathew said anything that got Lance into trouble, he wouldn't only cold-shoulder him in school. He would deny what Mathew had said. Perhaps he would claim that the fire had been entirely Mathew's idea and that Mathew was now trying to spread the blame! Lance might pretend that he had been the sensible one . . . and that Mathew had been acting big and had refused to listen to his warnings. It would be Lance's words against his! Everyone was sure to believe Lance. He was always so confident.

Unable to go back to sleep, Mathew wandered into the passage. The burnt smell hovered everywhere and the house felt strangely empty. No Mercy making beds and dusting. No Josiah humming hymns in the kitchen. No Mugo sweeping the veranda.

The door to the study was slightly open. Father was on the telephone.

'That's what I'm saying. I've no one. Only my Turkanas . . . No, I can't use them. They're my guards! I need new labour urgently . . . Smithers says I should get rid of the lot of them . . . Who should I contact?'

Mathew felt a new wave of dismay. Earlier this morning, he had seen Father remain grimly quiet while the inspector had his say. '*Once this has happened, you can't trust any of them. You see that now, Jack, don't you?*' Mathew remembered how Father had argued with Lance's father in the club. Yet now Father was quoting the inspector and was not even prepared to wait for the results of the screening! No wonder Mugo, Kamau and everyone else looked so distressed. They knew that they were innocent! Shouldn't he just go into the study and tell the plain truth? His shame and Father's anger would be quite terrible. But if he were a truthful boy, that's what he should do, shouldn't he?

'What are you doing, Mathew? I thought you were sleeping!' Mother startled him from behind. 'Since you're up, you can come to the kitchen and help prepare some vegetables.' She said nothing about his eavesdropping.

He accompanied her, relieved to have something to do. It saved him from making a hasty decision. There were beans to be stringed, potatoes and carrots to be washed and peeled. It wasn't nearly as easy as it looked when Mugo did it. Even Mother seemed a little clumsy when she offered to show him the best way to hold the peeler. Neither of them mentioned Josiah or Mugo. But however hard Mathew concentrated on his tasks, he couldn't stop himself remembering Inspector Smithers' barbed-wire prison. Did Mother and Father know about it? He dared not ask.

A little later, Father called them to the car. He was on his way to the dairy and needed their help with the morning milking. Before all this Mau Mau business, they would have walked to the dairy through the grove of pepper trees. But nowadays, Father drove even the shortest distances. Their route took them past the labour lines. Usually, there was some activity down there, even when the labourers were out in the fields. A woman or two would be busy washing clothes and always a handful of near-naked, pot-bellied little children would be playing between the long rows of wooden buildings. But today the lines were unnaturally silent. Only a couple of thin, mangy dogs lifted their heads and barked at the car. They looked hungry, roving around for food.

The Turkana guards saluted as they opened the gate to the dairy enclosure. Father stopped the car alongside the boma, where the cows stood restlessly waiting to be taken into the milking shed. There was no sign of Wamai, the old dairyman. Mathew hadn't seen him being herded on to one of the trucks, but his short, bent figure could easily have been submerged in the crowd.

'This is going to take us forever!' Mother sighed as she climbed out of the car. Father was already striding ahead and didn't hear. 'It's a long time since I've done this – and then it was for fun.' Mathew noticed how her right hand hovered close to her pistol holster.

Inside the milking shed, Father showed them the buckets and cloths for washing the cows' udders and teats, the milking pails, and the cooler cans into which the fresh milk had to be poured.

'Watch me do the first one,' said Father. 'If you make the cows nervous, the milk is affected.'

'You can show Mother. I know how to milk. I've done it with Mugo.' The moment that Mathew mentioned Mugo's name, he regretted it. Before Father could reply, he set off to bring in his first cow. If only he could work quietly in a far corner of the shed, on his own.

He talked to his cow as he had seen Mugo do when Wamai had let the two of them help him. Wamai had a Kikuyu name for each animal, like 'The one who was born early' or 'The one with the crooked leg'. But without Wamai, he didn't know his cow's name. However, Mugo's voice inside his head directed him. '*Be gentle with her. Tell her she is very good! Pull the teat like this. Two fingers, now all of them . . . squeeze!*' Mathew laid his head against the cow's flank, listening to the mild rumble in her stomach. He kept one foot against the pail just in case she took fright and kicked it.

He worked slowly, trying to get a steady rhythm in bringing out the milk and not being distracted by his parents and their fumbling. Even Father didn't seem to be doing as well as him. By just talking to the cows, one by one, Mathew could feel himself becoming calmer . . . and as long as he only remembered Mugo in the milking shed, he could push away the eyes and voice that said, '*You betrayed me.*'

They milked for over two hours. Waiting for Mother and Father to finish with the last two cows, Mathew walked outside and wandered to the back of the milking shed. A scurrying movement caught his eye, something small disappearing behind a bush. A child's foot? He was going to call Father but on an impulse decided to look himself. He stepped cautiously, however, towards the bush. A young boy, about six or seven years old, stared up at him in terror, crouched in the long grass.

'Habari?' Mathew asked. The child didn't reply. Did he not understand Swahili?

'Wĩ mwega?' Mathew remembered how Mugo had taught him 'How are you?' in Kikuyu. His captive looked so terrified that he wanted to reassure him. The child's mouth opened but he remained speechless.

'It's OK. Come with me.' Mathew reverted to English and to signs. The boy trembled as Mathew accompanied him into the milking shed.

Father immediately recognized him as a herd boy and, speaking in Kikuyu, he finally got him to talk. The boy had brought in the cows yesterday evening but he had been scared to return home because he was in some kind of trouble with his father. He had slept under a bush behind the milking shed, hidden from Wamai. In the early morning he had heard the commotion and realized something bad was happening. From his hiding place, he had seen the police take away the dairyman. The Turkana guards frightened him and he didn't know what to do. Father translated between the boy's short, nervous outbursts. Mother meanwhile poured some milk into a canister and gave it to him. He drank in long hungry gulps.

'What are you going to do with him?' Mother asked.

Father hesitated. 'I'll let Smithers know. I expect it depends what happens to his family. In the meantime, I'll ask the guards to feed him and keep an eye on him here. Until my new labour comes, at least he can help with the milking.'

Father took him to the Turkana guards at the gate. Neither the boy nor the guards looked happy at Father's arrangement but it was, nevertheless, agreed.

After lunch, Mathew helped Father clear out one of the barns to use as temporary stables. The horses were fretful and on edge. As Mathew listened to Father trying to put them at ease, he couldn't help thinking how Kamau would calm them. The stallion was always the most difficult. But Kamau knew how to say Jafari's name in a deep rolling way that made the stallion's ears prick up and his dark eyes steady. Kamau always talked to the horses in Kikuyu. Once he had told Mathew that they especially liked long Kikuyu stories. Kamau's eyes had laughed and Mathew had laughed too. Yes, Kamau's stories had always been the best. Without warning, Mathew was sobbing, face buried in his arms on a pile of hay.

'What is it, Mathew? What's the matter?' Father's questions came like rapid gunfire, dull at first then getting nearer. 'We're all upset, Mathew. We've just got to get on with it.'

He felt Father's hand brush over his head. But his sobs had taken hold of him.

'You – don't – understand! It's – all – my fault!'

'No, I don't understand!' Father sounded tired and irritated. Jafari was snorting in the background. 'You're overwrought and unsettling the horses. Go back to the house. If you've got something to explain, it will have to wait.'

Mathew forced himself up. With pieces of hay sticking to his clothes and his eyes blurred with tears, he fled. He had messed up everything and with everyone.

Later, faced with Father's questions in the study, he confessed. Father leaned against his desk and Mother sat in the winged armchair beside him. Both were silent while he blurted out the whole story. Mathew dared not look at their faces. Mother's would be anguished, while from Father he expected terrible rage. Instead, when his father finally spoke, his voice was cold and detached.

'This is all too late, Mathew. My stables and fields are burnt. You've done the damage and I'm left without labour.'

'But you have to tell Lance's father that Mugo and Kamau didn't start the fire! They're innocent!'

'Not according to the inspector.'

Mathew's forehead creased. *Whatever did Father mean?*

'Kamau never told me that his boy Gitau didn't go back to school this term,' Father said bitterly. 'Didn't say a word!'

'Lance's father suspects that he has joined a Mau Mau gang on the mountain,' Mother added with a heavy sigh.

'How does he know?' Mathew cried.

'Information from the home guards,' Father said tersely.

'Apparently they've spotted Gitau in the area and say he must be coming down here to get food from his family,' Mother explained. 'The inspector thinks Kamau and the others are part of a supply chain. Even Mugo might even have been smuggling food out of the kitchen!'

Mathew stared, dumbfounded, as Mother's right hand fiddled with the lapel of her shirt, then swooped to her lap where it rested on her pistol holster. It all sounded crazy. How would Mugo have got anything past Josiah?

'So you see, Mathew, the inspector would have been coming for them anyway,' Mother said in her wrapping-up tone.

'Smithers was right. I've been too trusting!' Father's fingers impatiently tapped the desk beside him. 'He reckons they've all taken the oath, the whole damn lot.'

Mathew's head hurt. His conscience had made him tell the truth. Yet Father was now telling him that Mugo and Kamau were guilty anyway. Loyal Kamau whom Father relied on more than any other worker . . . and Mugo, who had always looked out for Mathew . . . taken care of him . . . who had even tried to save him from disaster just yesterday! It was far too confusing. Mathew wanted to escape to his room, but Mother reminded him that there was still work to do. The cows were waiting for their afternoon milking. Any more delay and they wouldn't be finished at the dairy until after sunset when they should be securely indoors with everything bolted.

20

Breaking

When next Mugo opened his eyes, he was trembling on the hard concrete floor. He didn't know how long he had been there. An hour, a day . . . or more? A red hat was standing over him.

'Get up! You're lucky. The inspector is letting you go.'

Mugo didn't move as he struggled to take in what the man was saying.

'Haraka! Haraka!'

The red hat's foot began to dig into him. It took an effort to lift himself off the floor.

'Is my father coming?'

'You think the inspector is a fool? You won't see your father for a long, long time.'

'Where's he going?' Mugo cried.

'Detention.'

'Detention?' Mugo whispered in horror. Detention camps were the same as prison! There were stories of starvation, beatings and worse. It was said a person might disappear forever there.

'When the British soldiers get him, they'll find out everything he didn't tell the inspector.'

'But Baba isn't Mau Mau!'

'Ha! That's what they all say.' The red hat prodded Mugo with his baton towards the door. Mugo blinked at the light. The sun seemed to strike from behind a wooden watchtower that loomed high above the compound. The red hat pointed his baton at a truck parked beneath the watchtower, with people clustered in the open carriage at the back.

'Haraka! They are waiting for you.'

Mugo sprinted towards it, his legs unsteady. Drawing nearer, he saw the faces of his brother and sister staring down at him from the truck like scared, open-mouthed little masks either side of Mami. He recognized a few other labourers from Bwana Grayson's farm. Were they the only ones being sent back? Arms stretched down to help him clamber up. His brother and sister clutched at him and pulled him towards Mami.

'I thank Ngai that I see you. How is your father?' Mami's usually steady voice spilt like water from a breaking pot. Mugo heard her fear and hung his head. How could he describe Baba's awful cries?

'The red hat says Baba is going to detention, Mami.'

'I do not see him with the others.'

His eyes followed hers. On the left of the low

building where he had been locked up, enclosed in barbed wire, rows of men sat squatting on the ground with their hands stuck to their heads. Mugo's stomach cramped. Gitau had once told him how his teacher punished children by making them crouch like this. If you fell over, you were thrashed. Instead of the teacher with his stick, there were guards with guns encircling them. Were all these people going to this 'detention'? He would hate seeing Baba humiliated like a school child but it was even worse not knowing where he was.

'What have they done with your father?' Mami wrung her hands. 'No one here has seen him.'

Mugo glanced around him. There were mainly women and children and a few elderly men who looked withdrawn and dazed. Behind them, he glimpsed Mzee Josiah and Mama Mercy. Mzee Josiah sat on the floor with his head bowed with Mama Mercy leaning against him. Her eyes were closed and legs loosely splayed. Mugo hurriedly looked away.

'Mami, Baba was –' Mugo faltered. He had to tell Mami what he had heard, but the words stuck in his throat. Suddenly the engine spluttered and the whole truck shuddered. He had to show her the last place he had seen Baba before it was too late.

'See there, Mami!' He pointed to the line of doors in the building from which he had been released. One door was open but it was too dim to see inside. Had that been the room in which they had locked him? Could Baba still be lying in the one next to it?

'They put him in there, Mami!' He forced out the words as the truck shook its way towards the side of the building. All of a sudden other words were screaming out of him.

'You can't have Baba! Give him back!'

His cries were drowned by the roar of the engine. The truck was veering towards the right side of the building. They lost sight of the people being sent into detention. At the back of the building was a small courtyard with some huts on the far side. Two red hats were emerging from one of them. They were pulling something, someone . . . dragging someone between them. The figure's legs scraped along the ground. The head hung down, face to the ground . . . unrecognizable . . . but the jacket was unmistakably Baba's. Mami pulled the younger children close to her, turning their heads so they would not see. The shock seemed to run through her like lightning in a soundless storm. Tears surged mutely down her cheeks. Mugo buried his head against her. Grief and anger swelled inside him.

21

Cries at the Fence

Father's new labour took several days to arrive. He had instructed the labour agent that he wanted workers who weren't Kikuyu and had been obliged to wait for people to be brought down from the north. Father informed Mathew that he was no longer needed to help with the cows, hens, horses and vegetable garden, but he still had to assist Mother in the house. She had not been satisfied with anyone who said they could cook or do housework. Mathew suspected Father was only half listening as she complained at the breakfast table.

'There's no one who is a patch on Josiah or Mercy.'

'You will just have to train them up, then,' Father replied tetchily.

'You know I still can't believe that Mercy and Josiah really are Mau Mau.' Mother had already said this so many times it was like a refrain. 'It just doesn't seem like them.'

'Like it or not, that's Frank's information. Every

– single – worker – here – took – that – damn – oath!' Father's hand drumming the table made the willow-pattern china cups rattle on their saucers. 'Once they've taken the oath they can't be relied on.'

Mother was silent.

'At least Frank is not sending them to a detention camp – like our renegade Kamau!'

'But I can't imagine what they'll do in the reserve –'

'That's not our problem,' Father interrupted. 'We are not questioning Frank's judgement on this. His advice was clear. Don't take anyone back! Now I've got an entire new labour force to see to.' With that, Father left his tea on the table and strode out of the dining room.

Without his den behind the stables, Mathew found the best place to get away from the house was the strip of land that he used for target practice. It wasn't as hidden as his old hideout, but the orchard provided a screen. On the other side, you looked through the wire fence to the bush. It was where he and Mugo had found the fence broken . . . when his rashness and new Red Ryder had got them into trouble with an elephant. Mugo had saved him that day, not only from the elephant's anger but also from Father's. It seemed such a long time ago now.

Glad not to have to go to the dairy, Mathew began target practice but soon tired of it on his own. He wasn't concentrating properly and couldn't forget the argument at breakfast. When Father had said that Kamau was being sent to a detention camp, it was like a bombshell. Yet Father hadn't even stopped to talk about it. The fire had changed everything. Father suddenly trusted everything that Lance's father said just when Mathew could see that Lance was a mean, deceitful bully. He felt sick that he had ever wanted to be friends with him.

Laying his Red Ryder on the ground, Mathew sat on a tree stump and called Duma to his side. He fondled her ears.

'You're my only friend now, aren't you, girl?'

Duma raised her soulful eyes, wagging her feather-duster tail. Her copper-red coat glistened in the morning sun.

'You miss Mugo, don't you, girl?'

Duma's eyes and ears lifted expectantly and Mathew threw his arms around her neck, burying his face in her silky hair.

'He's not coming back, you know! Everything's gone wrong!'

Duma whimpered.

'I don't want to go back to school because I won't have any friends there now,' Mathew whispered. 'Lance will see to it.'

Duma startled him with a burst of loud woofs. Was she reacting to Lance's name? Then, just as abruptly, she turned and dashed to the fence, barking all the while.

'What is it, Duma? What's there?' Mathew picked up his gun and hurried after her. Duma was now scurrying alongside the fence. She seemed to be looking for a place to slip underneath. But the lowest wire was too close to the ground. She was now whining and barking alternately. Something must be there!

They were reaching the end of the orchard and the corner of the fence when Duma bounced ahead. She began to leap forward and back, in excitement and frustration. All of a sudden, Mathew saw why. On the other side of the fence, where the bush was cleared, was Kamau's homestead . . . and there, staggering out of the door with an upside-down stool and objects piled on top, was Mugo, with a hoe also clutched between his arm and chest.

'Mugo!' Mathew yelled spontaneously. Mugo halted and looked up towards him. So did Mugo's mother and two small children who were a few paces ahead, each laden with household objects. Mugo's glance was only fleeting.

'Haraka! Hurry up or you leave everything here!' A guard in khaki uniform emerged in the doorway behind Mugo. Even without the guard shouting,

Mathew knew that Mugo wasn't going to look at him again.

The family had almost reached the banana trees on the border of their compound when Mugo's mother unexpectedly turned and hastily stacked the pots that she had been carrying on top of Mugo's load. Steadying the box on her head with one hand, she began to run in the opposite direction towards the back of the house. The guard swished out at her with his stick but she didn't stop. Squawks and screeches rent the air and she soon reappeared with a hen under each arm. She scuttled at arm's length from the guard to catch up with her children. The squawking continued from behind the house.

New thoughts now occurred to Mathew. The hens could not have been fed since the fire! Whoever Father brought to replace Kamau would inherit the family's hens, their shamba and everything else that they had been forced to leave. In the reserve, there would be nothing. Mathew had some idea of what a reserve was like because when they drove to Nairobi they passed through a couple on the way. They were barren places where the cattle had eaten most of the grass and, unlike Father's cattle, their skin clung to their ribs. If the cattle didn't have much to eat, what was there for people?

Mathew felt his face burning. He had to see Mugo before they took him away! He had no idea what he would say but he just had to see him. He began to run. The quickest way was to cut alongside the house. But on the spur of the moment he slipped in through the French windows into the lounge, down the passage and into the larder. He could hear Mother in the kitchen. Holding his breath, he lifted the lid of Josiah's biscuit jar. It still had some soft crumbly butter biscuits . . . Josiah's speciality. Mathew took one of the brown paper bags that Josiah saved so prudently and, as quietly as possible, filled it with biscuits before sneaking back into the passage.

The first thing he saw from the front door was Father talking to a white officer next to a truck being loaded with people and possessions. They were on the other side of the security fence and the gates were shut. As Mathew ran to the gates, Duma came pelting towards him from the side of the house.

'Jambo!' he shouted to the Turkana guards. They stood with their ramrod backs to him. 'Open! Open please!' Duma echoed the words with barks.

But before the guards even turned to look at him, Father put up his hand, signalling 'No'. They were not to let him through.

'Go inside, Mathew,' Father called firmly.

'I want to say goodbye to Mugo . . . and to Josiah and Mercy!' He couldn't see Mugo. But there was

Josiah approaching the truck with his shoulders stooping forward and his head lowered. Mercy shuffled beside him. Each was laden with bundles. They had always kept their uniforms starched and spotless. Today their clothes looked dirty and crumpled as if they hadn't changed them for days. Since he had last seen them, they had become really old.

Father excused himself from the police officer and walked over to Mathew.

'There's no need for you to see this, Mathew,' he said briskly from the other side of the fence. 'Just stay inside like your mother, until it's over and done with.'

'But I *want* to say goodbye! I'll be quick.' He was beginning to whine. If he could only give Mugo the biscuits, Mugo would know that he was sorry and wished he wasn't going.

'We can't afford to let personal feelings come into this, Mathew. Go inside now!'

Father turned deliberately and walked back to the officer. Mathew's eyes prickled and he swiftly wiped the back of his hand across his face. Not doing what Father said would mean trouble later. But even before he could decide whether or not to defy Father, there was Mugo, behind Father, lurching towards the truck. With his load piled up to his chin, he had missed his footing. Mathew watched as Mugo swivelled like an acrobat, regained his balance and averted a crash. The sweat on his face glistened in the sun. In the past, Mugo would have grinned at his feat, but not today.

'Mugo!' Mathew cried. 'Over here, Mugo!' Once again Duma echoed him with barks. Mathew couldn't tell whether he was responding to him or to Duma, but Mugo slowly turned his head to look at them. Mathew felt those concentrated seer's eyes that could pick out the tip of a tail or an ear over a hundred feet away in the bush.

'I've got something for you, Mugo!' Mathew held up the brown paper bag. Father was already striding back towards him, but he fixed his gaze on Mugo, hoping desperately for a response. There was none. Mugo had clearly seen and heard him. Why did he give no reaction at all? Mathew lowered the bag, pressing his lips tightly to hold down his disappointment. Father came towards him, blocking his view.

'What have you got there?' Father sounded exasperated.

Mathew thrust the brown paper bag between the barbed wire.

'It's for – for Mugo!' he stammered. He jerked the bag up and, before Father could grasp it, the paper snagged on a spike. Josiah's best butter biscuits tumbled to the ground.

He heard Father sigh. 'Now will you go inside, Mathew? Maybe when you're older, you'll understand.'

Mathew stayed where he was, behind the barbed wire. He stared at Josiah's broken butter biscuits scattered on the dry red earth. Duma promptly scoffed up what she could reach. The ants would demolish the rest. Mathew's eyes blurred with tears. The truck's engine revved up, throbbing in his ears. He would probably never see Mugo, Josiah, Mercy again . . . or Kamau . . . If he didn't understand now, how would he understand later?

22

Burning

Dust rising up under the wheels invaded Mugo's throat and nostrils. Every bump and jolt rattled through the densely packed truck, jostling people up against each other and their belongings. He sat with Mami, Mzee Josiah and the children on a small mound of blankets. Mama Mercy lay at their feet on the metal floor, her head next to a cardboard box in which Mami had made some holes and put the hens. The only thing Mama Mercy would accept was a blanket from Mami for a pillow.

They were hurtling away from Kirinyaga. The great mountain of Ngai, and his ancestors, was already like a distant anthill. The mzungu had chased them from their home like a snake displaces ants. Everything had been left behind except what they could carry. The table and chair that had been Mami's pride, carried all the way from the second-hand shop in town . . . the wooden bed that Baba had built for her . . . the maize meal ground by Mami and carefully stored next to the tin of oil in the kitchen hut . . . the beans, tomatoes and greens ready for picking in the shamba . . . so much they had been forced to leave behind with the guards shouting in their ears 'Haraka! Haraka!'. In the panic he had even nearly forgotten his leather bag of treasures. *Yes*, he thought, *Gitau was right. Wazungu don't care when we suffer. We are insects to them.* He thought of Baba's legs dragging on the ground and winced. Baba could be lying on the floor of a truck like Mama Mercy, not even seeing where he was being taken. Baba had had a dream. His children would go to school and learn the wazungu's knowledge! They would learn how to get back their land! Wazungu would learn to respect them! '*They are people and we are people.*' Where was Baba's dream now? How would the prophecy of the great seer be fulfilled? Must his family be ants forever?

Mugo dug his knuckles into the blanket. To his surprise, Mzee Josiah clasped one hand over Mugo's fist.

'Your father – he's a good person,' Mzee Josiah said unexpectedly in his low gruff voice. Mugo was taken aback. It was as if Mzee Josiah knew what he was thinking. Baba and Mzee Josiah had never been close. Did Mzee Josiah not blame Baba in some way for their troubles? The inspector had surely questioned everyone about Gitau.

'This fire, it's bigger than all of us, my son.'

My son. Mzee Josiah had never called him that

before. Mugo felt the warm sweat of Mzee Josiah's palm on his skin.

'It will eat everyone – Kikuyu, wazungu, everyone.' Mzee Josiah withdrew his hand, slapping it on to his own thigh as if talking to himself as well as Mugo. 'But don't let the fire eat your heart! Do you understand?'

Mugo wrapped his arms around himself, pressing his wrists against his ribs. How could he stop it? The burning was already inside him, from his head to his stomach. The pain *was* in his heart. His mouth felt dry, too dry to speak. He sensed what Mzee Josiah was saying. He was telling Mugo not to hate. Perhaps he was even telling himself not to hate.

Mugo's eyes trailed the barbed wire alongside the road. One fence led to another. Wazungu were everywhere. A burst of barking made him turn his head. Behind the wire, three dogs, with spiky hyena faces, were chasing the truck. They looked as if they wanted to rip someone to pieces. He had seen Duma behind the bwana's fence, trying to reach him. She had only wanted to nuzzle him. But the bwana had kept her in. Mugo would have liked to scratch her one last time behind her long soft ears. The mzungu boy had been with Duma, calling his name '*Mugo! Mugo!*' How many times had he heard that? Today it wasn't in his bossy '*Hurry up, Mugo!*' or '*Play with me, Mugo!*' voice. It was pleading. But the bwana hadn't let him out.

Mugo had seen the boy holding up a packet. Even before he saw it tear on the wire and Duma snuffling her nose over the red earth, he had guessed it was a bag of Mzee Josiah's biscuits. When the boy used to sneak a batch of biscuits to eat in his den, he always slipped them into a brown paper packet. Afterwards Mzee Josiah's grumblings would reveal he was secretly pleased that his biscuits were so popular.

A sudden lump caught in Mugo's throat. It would have been better if the bwana had never taken him into his house and made him the kitchen toto! If he had stayed herding the cattle, he would never have got to know the mzungu boy whose grandfather had taken away his own grandfather's land. He had taught the boy how to make his first sling from goatskin. He had shown him how to make a ball out of banana leaves, a money box from bamboo, a snare out of sisal . . . all the things he would show a younger brother. When the boy had been silly or showing off, he had done his best to ignore it. He had looked after the boy like Baba said he had looked after the bwana when they had been children. So how could he ever forget the way the bwana had looked at Baba and him on the night of the fire, his eyes full of suspicion, accusing them of betraying him!

Did Gitau know what had happened to them?

Mugo could imagine his brother's enraged eyes narrowing as if to say: '*Now do you see? Now, do you understand?*' Mugo leaned over to a cooking pot and pulled out his small leather bag stuffed between some wooden spoons. He slipped his hand inside, his fingers pushing aside marbles given to him by the mzungu boy, a catapult, the piece of memsahib's china, and other childish treasures. When he pulled out his hand, his little wooden elephant lay upside down in his palm, its feet and tusks in the air. He revolved it with his fingers until the creature was facing him, trunk raised, tusks forward, ready to charge.

Mugo squeezed it in his palm, feeling the solid weight of its body carved out of Kirinyaga's wood. He prayed that Gitau was safe with Maina, and that his brother still kept the little elephant's companion with him. It was rough and dangerous up there in Kirinyaga's forests. When the long rains set in, pouring in torrents, it would be worse. Kirinyaga was now out of sight, no longer even an anthill. The truck was taking them somewhere far away, and Baba would be taken to some unknown place behind more barbed wire. Only the land would still join all of them to their mountain. They had been dug up . . . roots pulled out . . . and scattered like weeds to shrivel. *But the wazungu cannot dig up the land. It will always be here.* Wasn't that what Baba would have said . . . would say . . . if he could? As long as the land was there, they had to have hope.

Mugo glanced at Mami. His brother and sister had fallen asleep, their heads lolling against her. With her eyes closed against the dust, lines of worry cut her face like shadows on a mask. He had never thought of Mami as old. He was no longer a child. Without Baba, it was up to him now to take care of his family. But if he were called to join Gitau and the others fighting for *ithaka na wiyathi*, their land and freedom, would he not go? Mugo trembled at the burning tearing deep inside him. The fire was eating everyone and he did not know how to keep the blaze from his heart.

Afterword

It feels strange to stand in a place that appears so beautiful, calm and peaceful when you know that if the earth, grass and trees could speak they would tell you another story. This is what I have felt watching the morning mist rise up the slopes of Mount Kenya . . . Kirinyaga.

55,000 British soldiers were sent to Kenya during the Emergency, declared in October 1952. The Mau Mau killed thirty-two white settlers, although people who remember the news reports often say that 'it seemed like more'. Over 1,800 African civilians were murdered for being loyalists and hundreds disappeared whose bodies were never found. Many terrible stories were reported at the time. However, British forces killed at least 12,000 (possibly as many as 20,000) Mau Mau fighters and suspects.

The Emergency was a disaster for the Kikuyu people. Even families became divided. It was like a civil war. At least 150,000 Kikuyu men and women were imprisoned as Mau Mau supporters, most of them without any trial. If a hooded informer pointed a finger at someone, that was enough. Whole communities were punished as 'collective punishment'. The government extended the death penalty to cover a wide range of offences. People were sentenced to death even when the evidence against them was poor. 1,090 Kikuyu men were hanged and thirty women were sentenced to life imprisonment. There were far more executions in Kenya than in any other British colonial struggle. The government said that it had suspended human rights because of terrorism.

Some people in Britain protested strongly, like the socialist MPs Fenner Brockway and Barbara Castle who were active in the Movement for Colonial Freedom. Accounts of torture and abuse in the detention camps were published. But the British government backed its officials in Kenya, who kept giving in to the fears and demands of the white settlers. Even when there were charges, these usually resulted in very light sentences, such as three months' hard labour and a fine for burning a suspect's eardrums with lighted cigarettes or £25 for pouring paraffin over a suspect.

By 1957, there were no more fighters in the forests. The Mau Mau had been defeated, but the settlers wanted the Emergency laws to continue. In 1959, eleven detainees at Hola Detention Camp were clubbed to death by black guards while white warders watched. Officials tried to cover up the killings. But the truth came out and it led to a public scandal in Britain.

The Emergency was finally ended in January 1960. The British government prepared to hand over control to a government elected by all Kenyans. In 1963, barely ten years after my story ends, Jomo Kenyatta became the first prime minister of Kenya. A year later, he became President of the independent Republic of Kenya. A British governor had called him the 'leader to darkness and death' and he had been imprisoned for seven years during the Emergency. But, to help bring peace to his shattered country, Kenyatta declared, 'Let there be forgiveness . . . The hatred of the past should be forgotten . . . Let us build together in unity, not revenge.'

Although stories were passed on within families, and teachers taught Kenyan children an approved history of the struggle for independence, the Mau Mau remained a banned organization for forty more years until 2003. Even in 2005, I found that the National Museum in Nairobi had no displays of this painful past. I went in search of the Peace Museum in Nyeri. I had heard that it was a small room filled with objects, old documents and photographs donated by both rebels and loyalists. I especially wanted to see this memorial in which the stories from each side had been brought together under the same roof. However, the brave little museum no longer existed. There had been no money to keep it going.

Yet the ghosts of the past have a way of rising. In October 2006, lawyers in London launched a test case for compensation from the British government for a group of elderly Mau Mau detainees. Their claim is that torture and illegal abuse were part of the colonial policy to destroy their rebellion for independence. People are talking and writing more than ever. For years, stories have been hidden in hundreds of places . . . in forests and gullies, caves and

*homesteads, villages and towns. Many are now emerging
from the undergrowth of memory, breaking the silence.*

*In all this, I am only the storyteller who has to believe
that for Mathew, as for Mugo . . .*

kĩrĩ ngoro kĩrutagwo na mĩario . . .
the word in the heart is drawn out by talking.

Glossary

asante (*sana*)	thank you (very much)	Swahili
ayah	nursemaid	from Hindi
boma	cattle enclosure	Swahili
bwana	master	Swahili
bwana kidogo	little master	Swahili
fez	a pot-shaped hat	Turkish
habari?	how are you?	Swahili
hapana	no	Swahili
haraka	hurry	Swahili
irio	potato, greens, maize and beans dish	Swahili
ithaka na wiyathi	land and freedom	Kikuyu
jambo (short for *hujambo*)	hello	Swahili
kiboko	hippopotamus	Swahili
memsahib	madam, mistress	from Hindi/Arabic
mgunga	umbrella thorn tree	Swahili

mugumo	fig tree	Kikuyu
mzungu	white person	Swahili
ndio	yes	Swahili
ndovu	elephant	Swahili
panga	machete with a broad blade	Swahili
shamba	field, plantation	Swahili
syce	groom	from Arabic
toto (short for *mtoto*)	child	Swahili
ugali	stiff porridge made from maize meal	Swahili
wazungu	white people	Swahili
wĩ mwega?	how are you?	Kikuyu

KIKUYU AND SWAHILI NAMES

Baba	Father	Kikuyu/Swahili
Duma	cheetah	Swahili
Gitau	(no special meaning but identifies an age group)	Kikuyu
Husani	handsome	Swahili
Jafari	dignified	Swahili
Juma	born on a Friday	Swahili

Kamau	quiet warrior	Kikuyu
Karanja	(no special meaning)	Kikuyu
Kenyatta	from 'tao ya kenya' or 'light of Kenya'; Jomo ('burning spear') Kenyatta became Kenya's first African premier	Swahili
Kikuyu	a people of central/ southern Kenya	
Kipsigi	a people of the Rift Valley	
Kirinyaga	mountain of mystery (mispronounced by Europeans as Kenya, hence Mount Kenya)	Kikuyu
Maina	(no special meaning but identifies an age group)	Kikuyu
Mau Mau	underground Kikuyu movement of resistance against colonial rule	
Mami	Mother	Kikuyu
Mugo	seer or wise man	Kikuyu
Mugo wa Kibiru	a Kikuyu prophet	Kikuyu
Muhimu	young militant activists opposed to colonial rule	Kikuyu
Mzee	term of respect for an old man	Swahili
Ngai	God	Kikuyu

Njeri	daughter of a warrior	Kikuyu
Turkana	a people of northern Kenya	
Wamai	someone who loves water	Kikuyu

Acknowledgements

In 2004 I was invited to read my work and run writing workshops in Kenya as part of the UKenya celebrations for the fortieth anniversary of Independence from Britain. My thanks for the very diverse programme go especially to librarian activist Anne Moore and to Mark Norton, Information Officer at the British High Commission. It was during this visit, with its great contrasts, that I decided I would set a novel in Kenya. I knew it would be a challenge, remembering the extraordinary power of the novels of Ngugi wa Thi'ongo that I had first experienced some forty years ago. They were novels that took me beyond myself, into a world that I had not previously imagined.

I am most grateful to all those who have spoken to me about their memories of Kenya before Independence. In addition, my special thanks go to Fred Kinyanjui for his assistance on my second journey into the central Highlands. His conversations also made vivid the extreme dangers of being a Kikuyu child at that time. I am indebted to the work of many authors, including *Mau Mau from Within* by Donald L. Barnett and Karari Njama, *'Mau Mau' Detainee* by Josiah Mwangi Kariuki, and *Britain's Gulag* by Caroline Elkins. Space prevents me naming all the authors whose works have enlarged my understanding but my particular thanks go to David Anderson for his wide-ranging, insightful research in *Histories of the Hanged*.

I owe special thanks to Grace Gikonyo Kahende for her patient answers to my questions and her comments on my draft. I should also like to thank Maren Bodenstein, Jill Burger, Maya Naidoo, Madeleine Lake, the Maharasingham family, Praveen Naidoo, Olusola Oyeleye and offer particular thanks to Dr Fírinne NíChréacháin and members of *OYA!* in North London who shared their responses with me: Winifred Opoku, Adeoba Okekunle, Nancy Khanu, Jacinta Namataka, Joldin Olympio, Uju Nicola Ufomadu.

Finally, my warmest thanks as ever go to: my editor, Jane Nissen; my agent, Hilary Delamere; and to Nandha for his constant support.

Beverley Naidoo

Read on for a brand-new, exclusive interview with the Carnegie medal-winning author ...

Birthday   21 May

Hair   Could easily become a great grey bush, thanks to my East European forebears

Eyes   The colour of the sea at Zennor on a winter's day, thanks, perhaps, to my Cornish mermaid ancestor!

Children   Praveen and Maya

Pets   Once upon a time there were Flash Speedy Gonzales Naidoo, Hoppy and Daisy, Bubble and Squeak ...

Favourite place   The Dorset coast path or, perhaps, 6000 miles south on a ridge in the Magaliesberg

Deepest wish   May all weapons in the world be turned into musical instruments

What was the inspiration for *Burn My Heart*?

I think it was deeply layered but I found this among my first notes:

> *Story within story. Burying shame. Father and son.*
> *Man and boy. Friendship. Betrayal. Father buries*
> *story from childhood . . . But unearths it and tells it*
> *to son who is in process of betraying a friend.*

Burn My Heart began as a story that a father has buried. A guilty secret. In the course of writing, I removed this 'outer' story so that there is no visible narrator. My reader steps directly into 1951, shifting between Mathew and Mugo. However, the story at the core remains one that has been largely hidden under the dust of the past.

Power corrupts the truth as much by silence as by assertion. What do colonizers of other people's lands tell their children? What do they not tell them? How different are the stories told by parents whose lands are occupied and dominated? Our parents' stories help to shape us. Do you remember the first shock at hearing a story that contradicted a parent or trusted adult? Stories, like experience, can plant seeds of change. We do not have to be fixed.

Does the story relate to your own childhood and background?

I grew up as a white child in Johannesburg, South Africa, 2000 miles south of Kenya, at the time of the Mau Mau.

I would have heard what most children in Britain would have heard about terror and nothing about the struggle to regain land, equal rights and freedom.

I had an older cousin who had married and gone to live on a large farm in Kenya's Highlands. After Kenya's Independence, her family came to live in South Africa. Her youngest son, Neil, was born during the Emergency in 1953, the year when *Burn My Heart* ends. He was ten when they arrived in South Africa, where most white people continued to support white domination and apartheid. My cousin's family moved to the Cape and I didn't meet them at the time. It was 1964, the year that Nelson Mandela and his comrades were sentenced to life imprisonment. It was a time of arrests, detention without trial, and torture.

I was caught up in this but I was still a 'small fish'. I had been fortunate to have had my ways of seeing challenged by my older brother and university friends. I realized that if I didn't actively join the resistance, I would continue to be complicit in apartheid and its evils. My few weeks in jail were part of my education. For black South Africans the whole country was a vast jail. In 1965 my brother and various friends were set to spend several years in jail and I left for England. I thought I would be returning but my study abroad turned into twenty-six years of exile.

On 5 February 1982, I was listening to the BBC news when I heard that a twenty-eight-year-old doctor, Neil Aggett, had been found hanging in his cell at Police

Headquarters in Johannesburg. I rang my mother. Yes, it was Neil, my cousin's son. He had been working in hospital two nights a week and most of his time as an unpaid trade-union organizer. Although he was one of many detainees who died after torture by apartheid's brutal security police, he was the first white person to meet this fate. Desmond Tutu, then Dean of Johannesburg, conducted Neil's funeral service. Many thousands of black workers followed his coffin through the streets to the cemetery, singing songs of resistance and freedom just as they would have honoured a black comrade.

Who could have predicted this transformation for a mzungu child born into a settler family at the height of the Emergency in Kenya?

How did you feel when you won the Carnegie medal for *The Other Side of Truth*?

Disbelief at first . . . then utter elation! This was the first book with African origin and characters to have won the Carnegie in sixty-four years. In my acceptance speech I said: 'It matters to me deeply that in acknowledging this book, you are acknowledging the existence of a submerged world of refugees in our very midst. Equally, I am honoured that you are acknowledging my particular writer's map to provide a route into that world. I am very aware of how Africa, the continent of my origin, has shaped so much of my writing.'

What has been the response to your books from your readers?

I receive many letters from readers who appear to have been startled and moved. Often readers write, 'I didn't know that . . .' or they ask, 'Is it really true that . . .?' I reply that, although the wider situations are real, my characters are all imagined. Some readers, however, recognize experiences. A London schoolboy wrote to me after reading *Web of Lies*: 'The similarities between the lives of Femi and myself left me wondering. Wondering how two people can be so similar, wondering how you know so much about what young boys are going through . . .'

What advice would you give to young people who want to be writers?

Read the world! Don't confine yourself. Discover what extraordinary journeys can be made through ink on paper, including journeys into the mind and heart. Alert your senses to your own world around you. Observe the detail. Be curious, especially about people. Ask 'Why?' Keep a notebook. Play with words . . .

To find out more about Beverley Naidoo visit
beverleynaidoo.com

More stunning books from acclaimed author Beverley Naidoo

The children of an outspoken Nigerian journalist, Sade and her brother flee for their lives to England

Winner of the Carnegie Medal

'. . . an unforgettable novel' – *The Times*

Web of Lies
The moving sequel to *The Other Side of Truth*
'A compelling thriller' – *Books for Keeps*

Out of Bounds
An astounding, prize-winning collection about apartheid and South Africa

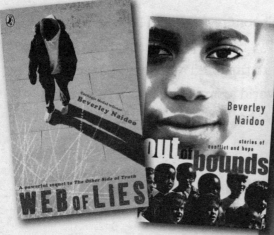

No Turning Back
Twelve-year-old Sipho escapes his violent stepfather by heading for the streets of Johannesburg in this heart-rending novel